# EVA CHASE

# REBEL DESTINY

TRAITOR OF VILLAINS

Rebel Destiny

Book 3 in the Traitor of Villains series



This is a work of fiction. Any resemblance to actual persons, living or dead, or actual events is purely coincidental.

First Digital Edition, 2021



Cover design: Christian Bentulan, Covers by Christian

Ebook ISBN: 978-1-989096-90-1

Paperback ISBN: 978-1-990338-21-2

❀ Created with Vellum

*Cressida*

The doctor took one last look at me before she started up the video chat on the laptop. Her frown told me that her final glance hadn't offered any new inspirations to solve my problems. I forced myself to lean back in the lightly padded chair as we waited for the call to connect, ignoring the knot in my stomach as well as I could.

I'd been in the Bloodstone University health center for over a day while the doctors and other medical staff examined me, prodded me, and spoke to each other in concerned murmurs. They had me in a small white room where they'd set up a cot so I had somewhere to sleep overnight—a room with walls that hummed with a faint sense of magical energy.

The space was shielded against magic coming in... or

out. Which I could understand them feeling was necessary, considering that as far as I could tell, I was essentially a walking magical bomb.

In the last twenty-four hours, I hadn't seen anyone except the health center staff, a couple of specialists they'd brought in from farther abroad, and Emeric, who'd been allowed to come in for brief visits between examinations. The isolation gnawed at me, but seeing the video chat window blink to a view of the current barons and scions filled me with more apprehension than anything else.

The rulers over fearmancer society were crowded around one side of a circular wooden table in a stone-walled room. It took me a second to recognize the details. The lines of a pentacle marked the table. I was looking at the barons' primary meeting room in the Fortress of the Pentacle, a space barely anyone other than barons past and present had ever seen.

Normally if I'd been going to talk with our rulers, many of whom had once also been my classmates, I'd have gone to the office room they'd set up here at the university. But because of my bomb-like status and the fact that the spell embedded in me seemed particularly keen on having me unleash its havoc on the people on the screen, it made sense for us to hold this conversation at a distance.

The barons' and scions' faces were small in the chat window, but I could tell none of them wore happy expressions. Even ever-optimistic Rory had a furrow in her brow. Noah, sitting between his brother and Connar, gave me a crooked smile and a little wave, but both gestures were stiff.

He'd wanted to come with me when the security staff had arrived to escort me to the health center after the spell had activated, but they'd held him back. I didn't think *he* was happy about the distance at all. But maybe that one thing could change for the better after this conversation.

"Hi, Cressida," Rory said in an apologetic and slightly wry tone. "This isn't how I was hoping we'd be talking next."

I shrugged, keeping up my unaffected front as well as I could. If Noah and Emeric hadn't been with me when the spell had kicked in, I might have blown up the entire pentacle of barons. I didn't think I was in a position to complain about a mildly unpleasant health-center stay. "It's all right. I'd rather you were over there and safe."

"How are you feeling?"

I paused to take stock of my physical state, just in case something had changed in the last couple of minutes. "Pretty normal. My tooth stopped hurting and the urge to go after you faded away after you all left the campus. I'm not sure exactly how long it took." I glanced at the doctor.

She consulted her notes. "Miss Warbury reported a total remission of the spell's noticeable effects at three-thirty p.m. Based on our records, all of the barons were at least ten miles beyond the campus boundaries at that point."

Noah nodded. "Right, that's when we got the go-ahead to get back to our work. Those of us who could, anyway."

His "work" was attending classes here on campus, which was a no-go zone for him at the moment, although he didn't really have any classes right now with the summer term just wrapped up and fall's not yet begun.

Next to Rory, Malcolm leaned forward, his intense gaze shifting from the doctor to me. My skin prickled with a fresh wave of uneasiness. The Nightwood baron was intimidating even through a computer screen.

"Have either of those feelings—the pain or the urge to go somewhere—come back since then?" he asked.

I shook my head. "Not that I've noticed. I guess it's possible something affected me when I was sleeping…" I trailed off, not totally sure of what time exactly I'd gone to sleep. The room didn't have any clocks, and the doctors had taken my phone.

"From approximately ten p.m. until six a.m. this morning," the doctor filled in. "Our monitoring spells didn't pick up any unusual activity during that time."

Malcolm hummed to himself and looked around at the others. "It doesn't kick in if only one of us is on campus, then."

The doctor's expression tightened. "Did one of you return during the quarantine? You were asked—"

Malcolm waved her protest off in his usual self-assured way. "It didn't seem likely to be a problem, considering as many as two or three of us have been at the university at the same time since Cressida came back. Yesterday was the first time we *all* were."

Declan picked up the thread with a typical even tone. "We wanted to test out whether that element had changed with the spell's activation, and we wanted to make sure your impressions weren't affected by knowing we were testing it. It seemed like a necessary step."

The doctor still looked unhappy, but she obviously wasn't inclined to argue with a room full of barons. "All right. I'll add that information to our records. During what time did you run this experiment?"

"Ten a.m. this morning, for a couple of hours," Rory said.

I wondered which of them had come, but they didn't say. I'd bet it'd been Rory. She'd have insisted on taking the risk, figuring out just how much of a risk *I* was—or wasn't.

She'd always been a better friend to me than I was sure I deserved.

Baron Killbrook, the oldest figure in the room by far, rubbed his mouth pensively. If he felt awkward surrounded by twenty-somethings and a couple of teenagers, though, he didn't let it show.

"What progress have you made in determining the structure of the casting and how it might be unraveled?" he asked.

Good question. The doctors hadn't bothered to fill me in on that subject in any detail so far.

The doctor with me shifted her weight on her feet, and I knew immediately that the news was bad. "It's a technique we're not very familiar with. The young man— Mr. Riplowe—who identified the spell was able to enlighten us on some of the strategies his, ah, former colleagues had been experimenting with, but his understanding was limited. At the moment, testing it both

magically and physically has revealed certain instabilities…
It seems likely that casting any aggressive magic on it or
attempting to remove the object containing it will only
eliminate the spell by setting off its intended effect."

She was trying to sound polite about it, but I could
follow that explanation just fine anyway. She meant if they
tried to pick apart the magic the reapers had cast into my
tooth—or attempted to simply take out the tooth—it'd
explode right then, whether the barons were around
or not.

In other words, if they tried to remove the casting, it'd
murder me.

My throat constricted. I'd known that was possible,
even likely. The reaper families had cast a similar spell on
Emeric's iguana familiar, and he'd had to kill it to stop the
spell from killing us first. But that had been in a tense
situation when every second counted. Deep down, I'd
kind of been counting on the best magical medics in the
country being able to come up with a different solution.

On the other side of the screen, Noah's face darkened
even more. "There has to be a way to get it out of her," he
said. "She can't just live with their magic keeping its hold
on her forever."

Or die with it, he didn't have to add.

"We're trying every approach we've had any success
with in the past," the doctor assured him, her voice
strained. "We've only had a day to work on it. With more
time, we'll have a better chance of coming up with a
solution. Until then, I think it's best if you continue to
take appropriate precautions…"

My head jerked around. "You can't be telling the barons that they're not allowed on campus as long as I'm here. This is one of their main bases of operations." It was one of the few places in our world where they'd been pretty much safe, with the protection of the school's powerful wards holding back the mages who wanted to overthrow them… until now.

"We could prepare a suitable space for Miss Warbury off-campus," the doctor said with obvious hesitation.

"No," Declan said. "That would only make her and everyone working on the case vulnerable to attack. If the reapers realize we've uncovered their plot, they may try to simply destroy her rather than allow you to continue to study their magic."

I'd have felt warmer toward him for the vote in support of my safety if I hadn't suspected the academically-minded baron was at least as concerned about losing the data the doctors were gathering on the spell as he was about losing me.

"But the rest of you," I started, not really knowing how I was going to finish that sentence.

Malcolm jumped in. "We'll work around it. We know that so far the casting has only taken effect when all of us barons are on campus at the same time. We can still come and go individually. As long as we steer clear of the health center, there really isn't much risk, is there?"

The doctor's lips pursed. "I suppose not. To the best we can determine, the radius of the explosive effect would be limited to approximately a hundred feet, with it only being fully destructive much closer by, and of course the protections on this room—"

Rory set her hands on the table, fixing the doctor with a dark gaze that could be equally intimidating in its own right. "I don't think Cressida should have to lose all her freedom over this. Classes are about to start up. She isn't a danger to anyone other than us in the pentacle. If we need to come to the university, we can let you know and she can go to the health center then, but otherwise I think she should be allowed free access to the campus."

She, I knew, was looking out for my wellbeing above everything else. I shot her a quick smile. "It's okay, really. I understand—"

"No," she said firmly. "The reaper families already put you through enough of an ordeal. We're not going to add to it. You were living on campus just fine for two weeks before the spell became a problem; there's no reason you should have to live like a prisoner from now on."

The other barons around the table nodded. "That's reasonable," Baron Killbrook said.

"We don't know if the effects of the casting might escalate," the doctor pointed out.

"Then we can adjust our approach if it does, can't we?" Connar said. "Cressida can tell you if she notices that it's affecting her more."

"Of course," I said quickly. "I'd have done that anyway."

The doctor sighed. I suspected she was mainly frustrated about losing easy access to her test subject. "All right. Once we've finished conducting the next phase of tests, we'll mostly need to research techniques and run trials on experimental spells of our own construction. But I do think Miss Warbury should undergo some additional training in mental control so that she'll be more able to defend against the spell's compulsion if it comes over her again. Given the strength of the casting, I doubt she'd be able to break its hold completely, but she could buy herself time to give a warning to those nearby."

"I'd be happy to do that," I said. I'd be happy to do anything that made it less likely I'd end up blasting apart like human TNT, really.

It figured, didn't it? I'd thought I was going to head out to Portland, investigate the reaper families, and do something good to pay back the barons for their acceptance and support after I'd cut ties with my parents. Instead, I'd been tricked, humiliated, and now returned to them as a much bigger threat than I'd ever been before. My parents and their allies had turned me into a weapon against the people who'd stood by me the most.

The thought made my stomach churn. But what could I do about it now? Nothing other than deal with the situation as well as I could, which had basically been the story of my life since I'd sided with Rory and the other scions against the old barons. The story of my entire life, actually, since life under my parents' authority hadn't exactly been a walk in the park either.

I didn't know the words were going to spill out until they were already tumbling off my tongue. "I'm sorry about all this. I had no idea—the reapers must have done it after they knocked me out—I didn't even know it was *possible* for them to cast a spell like this—"

Rory's eyes widened with concern. "It's all right. How could you have known? No one blames you. We just want to make sure you can get through this okay. We *will* make sure of that."

I wasn't sure everyone around her shared quite the same commitment to my survival, but it was a relief to hear her say that, even if the relief came with a pang of guilt.

"I'll start the mental training right away," I said. "Professor Razeden would probably know a lot of good techniques." He specialized in helping us control our fearful emotions, so why not controlling other impulses as well?

The barons started to stir with the recognition that the meeting was coming to an end. Noah sat up straighter, catching my eyes through the screen. "I'll come right back —maybe I'll even get there before they release you from the health center so I can—"

Even as my heart leapt at the thought of seeing the guy I loved in person again, Declan grasped his brother's shoulder. "It isn't wise for any of us to be near Cressida until this situation is sorted out."

Noah frowned at him. "But—"

"We can talk about this between ourselves." Declan nodded to us. "Thank you for making this call."

Then the screen went black, cutting me off from my boyfriend entirely. I swallowed thickly.

Noah wasn't even a baron yet—he wouldn't take on

the title until after he'd graduated. But I supposed it was true that I was a potential threat to him too. How long would it be before I *could* really see him again?

Would I *ever* get to?

Just like that, my parents and their co-conspirators might have ruined my life in even more ways than they'd hoped to.

2

Noah

As Jude shut the laptop, I spun in my chair toward my brother. "I'm not staying away from Cressida for the entire time she's dealing with this spell, which could take ages for all we know. I was *with* her when it took hold the first time. She didn't try to do anything to me at all—it was only sending her toward the actual barons."

Declan fixed me with the serious older brother look I was way too familiar with. "You're going to be a baron soon. We have no idea what elements the reapers worked into their casting. It could switch to targeting you at any time—and if you're right there next to her, you won't have time to protect yourself."

Even though what he said made total sense, my jaw clenched. She was my girlfriend, for fuck's sake. Did he figure I should just break up with her because of a casting that wasn't remotely her fault?

"She's going to do the additional mental training so she'll be more in control," I pointed out. "And I can—I don't know—make sure never to be totally helpless around her, like falling asleep in the same room or whatever." I'd gotten used to enjoying the sensation of waking up next to Cressida over the last several days, which was all the time we'd had so far to enjoy the relationship she'd finally felt comfortable pursuing, but I could live without that small pleasure for a while if the alternative was never seeing her in person at all.

"It won't be a guarantee," Declan said. "And the spell is never going to be completely under her control. For all we know, the reapers can set off the explosive effect from afar whenever they want. Any time, they could decide to cut their losses and take out whoever they can."

"What if I don't mind taking that risk?"

Declan sighed. "Noah…"

"I'm sorry," Rory spoke up in her softer but equally firm voice. "I agree with Declan. For now, at least. I know how hard it's going to be for you—and her too—and I don't want to get in the way of your relationship, but we know so little about what the spell even involves right now." She glanced around the table at the other barons. "I do think Noah and Agnes should be allowed to go back to classes. We'll just have to make sure that their schedules don't align with Cressida's—that they're never in the same room or a room very close to her."

My heart sank. Rory was the closest to Cressida out of

everyone here other than me. If even she was going to take the side of extreme caution, I didn't have much ground to argue from.

"It might not be that long, right?" Jude said in his typically breezy way, flopping into a chair at the other side of the table. "The health center and whatever other doctors they're bringing in could have this all figured out in just a few days."

His uncle nodded. "And even if they can't remove the spell that quickly, we'll continue to increase our understanding of it so we can better judge the risks."

I let out my breath in a huff, groping for another, better response, but before I could, Agnes cleared her throat. As the youngest person from the barony families to attend these meetings, she didn't insert herself into our conversations often. We all paused to hear what she had to say that she'd felt was worth putting a voice to.

She hesitated for a second, her expression uncertain, and then said, "It's not just about us, is it? If being near Cressida ends up triggering the spell in her, then it could hurt a whole bunch of people around us too. We can't decide just for ourselves when the risk affects everyone on campus."

Oh. She was right, and I'd been too caught up in my determination to be there for Cressida, to be *with* Cressida, that I hadn't even considered that factor. My face heated.

"Of course," I said before anyone else needed to jump in and agree. "I should have kept that factor in mind. It's definitely not worth testing the spell's limits in any way that could threaten the other students."

Declan grasped my shoulder with a reassuring squeeze. "I know how much she means to you. The doctors are doing everything they can, and when we know more about the casting, we may be able to relax some of the precautions. And you can talk to her by phone or computer without any problems."

It wasn't exactly the same, but I knew he knew that. I gave him a tight smile. He was doing his best. We all were. It was just an awful situation.

At least the barons weren't insisting that I not even set foot on campus. I suspected the fact that I was more protected there behind the wards than I was anywhere else in the world factored into Declan's acceptance of Rory's proposal. I'd be somewhat close to Cressida. Even if I couldn't make a case for seeing her in her dorm or wherever, once the doctors had been working on the problem for another day or two, I might be able to swing an argument to visit her in the sealed room where they'd been running their tests.

It wouldn't exactly make for a passionate reunion, but it'd be better than nothing.

The barons had continued the conversation around me while I'd resigned myself to their verdict. They were discussing some other expert in aggressive magic that they could ask to come over from Spain. I didn't know anything about the guy Hector Killbrook had suggested, but my mind darted to the other ways *I* might be able to speed along a solution to the mess the reapers had created.

Back when we'd been investigating the reaper families in Portland, Cressida and I had arranged for one of the Nary students at Blood U to hack into a business computer and download a bunch of files. I knew the barons had gone through them with Brandon after the reapers had kidnapped Cressida and me, but they hadn't had as much firsthand knowledge about the situation as I did—and they hadn't known we'd be dealing with a spell like this. Maybe there'd be something in his findings that'd point us in a useful direction.

When the meeting wrapped up, I hurried out to my car to make the drive back to campus as quickly as I could. On the walk over, I sent Brandon a quick text. He'd gone home for a few days during the break from classes, but I'd seen him returning to the dorms yesterday. Hopefully I could track him down without too much trouble.

Kato scampered over from roaming the grounds around the Fortress and hopped into the passenger seat next to me. He looked at me curiously as if he could tell I had a lot on my mind, but it wasn't as if the raccoon could really understand what we were up against. I settled for giving his fur an affectionate ruffle that he seemed to appreciate.

The campus was still pretty deserted with classes not starting for another couple of days. Only a handful of cars sat in the stalls in the parking garage. I resisted the urge to park next to Cressida's Mustang to have an excuse to maybe bump into her—not that she was going to be allowed to go for any drives anytime soon.

The health center hadn't alerted us that they'd released

Cressida from their testing yet, so for the moment, I could roam pretty freely. Declan was already arranging for me to stay in an unused apartment in the professors' section of Killbrook Hall until I could "safely" return to my usual dorm once Cressida was back in hers, just a floor above mine. The way the barons had been talking, they were going to structure our time pretty tightly to ensure Agnes and I never got too close to her. It was going to be a fantastic start to fall term, that was for sure.

But sarcasm aside, I'd rather be here with restrictions than not here at all.

Brandon had replied to my text sometime during my drive. I tapped a quick response to let him know I'd find him in his dorm room and was at the door five minutes later.

He answered my knock with his laptop already tucked under his arm. "I've got the files ready to go. I don't know if there's anything that'll be useful. I combed through this stuff pretty thoroughly with the barons while you were missing."

And as far as we knew, the Portland reapers had only been vaguely aware of the kind of magic the higher families had cast on Cressida as well as Emeric's familiar. But they'd been trying to get in good with those higher families however they could. They might have stumbled on something that would give us a clue without even realizing the significance.

"It can't hurt to look," I said. "Let's see what you got."

Brandon plopped down on the sofa in the middle of the dorm common room, and I took the chair across from him. He popped open his laptop with a snap, his fingers flying over the keys practically the second he had it open. It never ceased to amaze me how easily he interacted with the device. I mean, I'd used plenty of computers in my time, but never to the point that I knew what I needed to be clicking or typing without ever stopping to think.

"I grabbed a lot of stuff from the Achelings' computer," he said without missing a beat. "Some of it was personal business stuff, but a bunch was at least tangentially related to these other, rich families that I guess are against your current magical rulers?"

Because he was a Nary—someone without any magical ability—we hadn't gotten too deep into explaining the workings of our world even after it'd been exposed to him. He'd never seemed all that interested in the political side, to be fair.

"Yep," I said. "They supported the old barons and are pissed off that the new ones took their place with attitudes a lot more friendly toward people like you, among other things. They're the ones who cast this spell on Cressida that's fucking everything up. So anything to do with them would be our best bet of finding answers."

Brandon hummed thoughtfully and tapped some more, I assumed sorting through the files. "Thankfully the Achelings were fairly organized. These people were apparently keeping as close tabs as they could on the more powerful families—there are notes, photographs like they were stalking them, the works. From what I've heard, they were trying to find out enough about what the prominent families were planning to be able to offer an inside edge, get in good with them. I don't get the impression that worked out so well."

I shook my head, grimacing. "No. So maybe they didn't find out enough that would help us either. Still… What activities did they note down?"

"Let's see… Various sightings at financial institutions, coming and going from their own businesses—which isn't exactly surprising… Trips to different properties… The barons wanted all the records on that, but I don't think they turned anything up. That was when they were trying to figure out where you'd gotten kidnapped too."

None of that sounded promising. "Anything else?" I asked.

Brandon nodded. "Oh, sure. Clothing shopping, meetings in some kind of office building that of course the person taking the pictures didn't have access to. They took notes on which people were meeting with whom, but it didn't seem like the barons got anywhere with that either. Dining out, animal purchases, someone installing a new fence around—"

"Wait," I broke in. "Animal purchases? What's that about?"

Brandon clicked a few times and contemplated the screen. "Right, I remember going through this with one of the barons. There's a business in New York state that sources animals for magical uses—mostly ideal familiars, I gathered? The Achelings' sources had a couple of different records of the major families coming by to make what looked like major purchases." He paused. "Cressida's last name is Warbury, right?"

My heart skipped a beat. "Yeah. Why?"

"Her parents came around that place once too. It doesn't mean anything—they went a lot of places. But I remember the barons were interested because no one would normally need that many familiars all at once, so they wondered what they were up to. But they questioned the family who owns the business—the Millbanes—and didn't get anything incriminating from them. I think they concluded that whatever the bad guys were up to, the animal sellers didn't know."

My pulse started thumping again, a little faster than usual. Suddenly all I could think of was Emeric's familiar, the iguana he'd protected so carefully and then had to kill so brutally when the reapers had turned it into a weapon against us.

To perfect a spell, they'd have needed a lot of test subjects, wouldn't they? And for a spell they wanted to be able to embed in human beings, they'd need *living* test subjects.

The name Brandon had mentioned had triggered a twinge of recognition too. "Millbane?" I said. "Is there a student at the university from that family?"

Brandon's eyebrows rose. "Actually, there is. The baron who was talking to me about this stuff mentioned her too —a daughter, twenty years old. I'm sure they questioned her too. It doesn't seem like she was helpful."

But back then, the barons hadn't known everything they should be asking. I'd have to look up her first name and then whatever else I could find out about her. But first—

I motioned to Brandon. "I want to hear every detail the Achelings took down about the animal purchases, even if it doesn't sound relevant at all."

Most if not all of those creatures had probably died serving the reapers' purposes. But maybe if I followed this lead right, Cressida wouldn't have to meet the same fate.

3

*Cressida*

"Again," Professor Burnbuck said with a flick of his fingers toward me.

At the same moment, Professor Razeden opened his mouth to intone his persuasion casting for what felt like the millionth time. I braced myself automatically, my feet firm against the floor in the black, domed room where he usually carried out our desensitization sessions. The solid darkness of the walls, the still air, and the silence made it easy to narrow all my focus down to the impact of his spell.

"*Walk to me,*" he said, magical energy twined through his dry voice.

Under normal circumstances, I'd have concentrated on strengthening my mental barriers against the casting so that it didn't impact me at all. Illusion might be my specialty, but I wasn't bad at persuasion—I probably couldn't have fended off the professor completely, but I might have been able to get away with only taking a step or two rather than walking all the way over to where he was standing on the opposite side of the room.

But practicing my shielding wasn't going to help me fend off the effects of the spell already embedded in my head. Or, at least, we didn't want to count on the approach working. We couldn't exactly test the possibilities without putting the barons in jeopardy. So I'd spent the afternoon letting Professor Razeden's spells take hold and then honing my ability to resist their effects.

The energy of his casting tickled into my brain. I immediately blanked my mind, picturing nothing but the black wall behind him, imagining I had no idea where Razeden even was—so of course I couldn't walk to him. The strategy had sounded kind of ridiculous when Professor Burnbuck, the university's illusions expert and my senior mentor, had suggested it alongside the others we'd tried, but it'd actually worked out the best.

In a way, it was an illusion of its own. I was doing my best to convince myself of an alternate reality where the persuasive casting's call couldn't be answered. Considering how much I favored illusionary magic, it probably made sense that my mind responded well to this tactic.

The effect wasn't perfect, though, at least not yet. *There are just black walls all around me, no sign of the professor,* I told myself firmly, picturing a room with no one but me and Burnbuck in it, but the spell dug its claws into my will anyway. The muscles in my legs and hips twitched with the growing urge to move. Pain prickled over my scalp.

I took slow, even breaths, repeating my mantra of denial over and over in a corresponding rhythm. The urge and the pain didn't go away, but they crept up on me slower than ever before. I held my legs stiffly still, refusing to give in.

I had to show I could control this kind of compulsion —control it for more than a minute or two. The doctors and other experts who'd finally finished prodding me in the health center had made that a condition of my being allowed to return to somewhat regular life on campus.

It could have been minutes slipping by or only seconds. The boredom of this standoff made my resistance harder—but there was no guarantee I'd have anything fascinating to distract me if the reapers' spell took hold. I had to be ready for the toughest possible challenge.

*There are just black walls all around me, no sign of the professor.*

The room was mildly cool, but sweat started to bead on my forehead. A droplet trickled down my back. An ache was spreading through my thigh muscles. I resisted the impulse to close my eyes against the growing discomfort. I'd already discovered that avoiding sight actually made it harder to fight the persuasion. I couldn't convince myself I was seeing something I wasn't—or not seeing something I was—if I couldn't see anything at all.

Finally, the prickling sensation that'd wrapped around my head condensed into a sharper pinching. My lungs constricted, my breaths becoming a struggle. My knees wobbled. Then my left foot jerked forward, planting itself on the floor a pace ahead of me. I gritted my teeth, but my right foot followed a few seconds later.

I would have fought each step the entire way across the room, but Burnbuck held up his hand to call an end to the test. "*You can stay where you are,*" Razeden said, and his previous spell's grip fell away.

As the compulsion to walk fled me, my shoulders sagged. It'd always been a bit of a shock when the effect released, but this time even my bones felt as if they'd turned into jelly, and my head had gone so light I had the impression it might float away from my body.

I dragged a deeper breath into my unconstrained lungs and let myself move to the nearest wall so I could lean against it. Really, I wanted to sit right down on the floor for a minute, but I'd rather not look any weaker than I already did.

Of its own accord, my tongue veered to prod my traitorous tooth. It hadn't given any sign of being at all different from my other teeth in the time since the spell had activated. It hardly seemed fair that something that was threatening to destroy my entire life—totally literally —could act so innocent.

"That was very good," Professor Burnbuck said, with enough appreciation in his tone that I believed he meant it. A rush of relief swept through me before he'd even continued. "That time you held out for nearly half an hour. Plenty of time to give a warning and ensure anyone at risk could remove themselves from danger."

Everyone except for me, of course. His gaze caught

mine, his mouth tensing for a second, and I suspected he was considering the same thing.

There was no way for me to escape the magical bomb the reapers had constructed inside me unless someone around here figured out how to unravel that spell. Or at the very least, how to remove the tooth they'd hidden the casting in without setting the explosion off.

Burnbuck ran his hand through his scruffy hair, which only looked more rumpled afterward. "That performance more than satisfies the requirements we were given. We don't want to exhaust you. We can pick up with additional practice to continue to strengthen your resistance tomorrow. Although we should probably discuss methods of warning and that sort of thing now." He nodded to Razeden. "Thank you for your help."

Razeden offered a slight smile in response, but his expression was solemn. "You can finish up whatever you need to discuss in here, and I'll be available tomorrow. The first desensitization sessions won't start until Monday."

He left, shutting the door behind him. Burnbuck gave me a thoughtful look and said, "Why don't you sit down?"

Apparently I hadn't been maintaining the appearance of steadiness as well as I'd intended. I grimaced but accepted his suggestion, sinking down to the floor with my back still braced against the wall.

"All of this is just a stop-gap measure," I couldn't help saying. "It isn't a long-term solution."

"I'm sure the doctors and their consultants are working hard at coming up with something that'll remove the danger completely," Burnbuck said. "With a new type of spellwork, it takes time to figure out the best way to tackle it."

"What if it took the reapers *years* to come up with the idea and make it feasible? Doesn't that mean it'll take just as long for anyone else to work it out?"

Burnbuck eased down onto the floor kitty-corner to me, folding his legs in front of him. "Not necessarily. I wouldn't say that's even likely. They were starting from scratch, and we have an example of the spell right in front of us to examine." He paused, running his hand along his narrow chin. "I know this situation must be scary and frustrating, but keep your spirits up if you can. If only because it'll make things easier for you in the meantime."

I might have been annoyed by the advice if I hadn't known how genuinely he meant it. Professor Burnbuck wasn't the most demonstrative guy, but it was obvious he cared about his students. He'd never hesitated to set aside whatever he was doing if I came to him asking for help with a particular strategy I was struggling to perfect. And he'd gotten into the habit of regularly checking in on me and the other students under his mentorship in the past couple of years since the battle with the barons, just to touch base in general and confirm we were getting by all right.

I studied him for a moment. He had plenty of gray flecked through his messy hair and the shading of beard along his jaw, and faint crow's feet marked the corners of his eyes. I'd figure he was about fifty, around the same age as my parents and the older barons. He'd have grown up with them, gone to school with them, had them rule over him and the rest of the students as scions on campus the way Malcolm and the others had used to lord their authority over us.

"You must have known a lot of the reaper families pretty well," I ventured. "From when you were in school and then their kids coming here while you've been teaching. Bloodstone University was a key aspect in a lot of the old barons' plans, so having as many professors on their side as they could manage would have been to their advantage. Did they ever try to 'recruit' you into the fold?"

One corner of Burnbuck's mouth twitched upward, forming a slanted smile. "Oh, yes. I'd imagine they made the rounds with everyone in a position of any influence. I can't say I knew the specifics or the extent of what they were planning, but it was clear they wanted to shore up as much support as they could for moves they knew might meet some resistance."

But he hadn't joined them, obviously. He'd sided with Rory and the others from the start.

I opened my mouth and then closed it again, trying to figure out how to phrase my question without sounding utterly pathetic. In the end, I decided that there was no way to do that, so I might as well just spit it out.

"How did you… How did you manage to stay out of all that and not have them ruin your life?"

Something in Burnbuck's expression softened in a way I didn't normally see. He glanced away for a moment, his forehead furrowing, as if he was thinking back to the times I was asking about.

"You have it harder than I did," he said when he met

my gaze again. "And I'm sorry that you do. By the time they made any real overtures with me, I was fully independent with a good job and the headmistress's respect to ensure I kept that job. And my family has never been particularly entwined with that of any of the barons other than I was decently good friends with Hector Killbrook during our school days, but that obviously wasn't a point of leverage before."

"So they just didn't try that hard to convince you," I filled in.

"To some extent. You've become a target in part because of your parents' feeling they have the right to dictate your loyalties, and in part because of how closely they worked with the old barons. I was starting in a relatively neutral position, being asked to pledge a new allegiance. I'd imagine that in the eyes of a lot of the remaining reapers, you betrayed allegiances already made. Never mind that you didn't have any choice in who your parents associated with."

"Yeah." I swallowed thickly. "They definitely see me as a traitor. That was made *very* clear even by the lower-level families in Portland."

Burnbuck inclined his head. "But you're not. *You* know that, don't you? When you were old enough to see the situation clearly and make a decision for yourself, you made your first real choice then. The rest had nothing to do with you, no matter what they think. You don't *deserve* this, Cressida."

I hadn't known I'd want to hear those words, but somehow they choked me up in an instant. It took me a second to find my voice again. "Even if they weren't that hard on you, there must have been pressure. How did you… not care, or whatever?"

He lifted his shoulders in a slight shrug. "I'm not going to sugarcoat it and pretend it was easy. I had to fend off attempts at threatening my job, even my life, though not as extreme or overt as what you've gone through. But in the end, they're bullies, and bullies only maintain their power by convincing other people of it. If you refuse to believe in them, they lose that power."

"To some extent," I said with a wry edge I couldn't restrain. "Some of that power is very real."

"And the situation they've put you in is horrible. But I do think we'll get you out of it, and what happens from there is at least as much up to you as it is to them." Burnbuck paused. "You're already starting to learn that one of the best illusions we can conjure requires no magic at all. That fact applies to more than just resisting this spell. If you act as if things are the way you want them to be, sometimes you can convince enough people of it— including yourself—to make those things actually real. Be a woman the reapers and your parents can't touch, even if you're shaken inside… and you'll be much closer to having that be true."

I didn't know how well I could put those instructions into practice, but his support loosened a little of the tension I'd been holding inside me. I flexed the muscles in my legs and found that they felt ready to support my weight again. Pushing to my feet, I aimed a small smile at my mentor. "Thanks. For doing all this practice with me, and for the pep talk."

He smiled back. "Any time."

"What was it you wanted to discuss about proper warnings and all that?"

Burnbuck waved off the question. "I think simply telling anyone within hearing that they should keep their distance and call in the health center staff should be enough, as I'd imagine you could already figure out."

He'd given that excuse so I had the chance to talk to him alone rather than having Professor Razeden hear my insecurities come out too. "Thank you," I said again. "When do you want to get started tomorrow?"

"I'll see you here at… should we say ten o'clock? I'll check with the barons just in case."

I nodded. "That sounds fine."

As I climbed the steps to the ground level of Nightwood Tower, my phone pinged in my pocket with a text that'd come in during my time in the desensitization room, where cell signals didn't reach. I pulled out the phone, and a flutter ran through my pulse when I saw the message was from Noah.

He couldn't resist getting in a flirty comment even when he was mostly looking to talk business. *Missing you, mon petit chou-fleur. I've got a lead on someone who might have some answers for us. Do you remember Hadley Millbane? I've looked at the school records, and she was in the same junior dorm as you for a couple of years. Her family appears to have been involved in supplying animal test subjects to the reapers while they were developing their new magical technique. I thought you might want to have a chat with her, if you were friendly at all.*

"Friendly" wasn't exactly the word I'd use for my acquaintance with Hadley Millbane, but a sense of purpose stirred inside me, fueled both by the opportunity and Professor Burnbuck's recent words.

*Send me the details,* I wrote back. *I'll go have a chat with her right now.*

4

*Cressida*

I hadn't really talked to Hadley since I'd moved from the junior dorms to the senior residence building. She was a year younger than me, so we hadn't had any classes together for a while after that either, and by the time she'd moved over to the senior side after the battle with the barons had gone down, my social priorities had been… pretty different from what they were before.

As I psyched myself up for the chat she'd seemed hesitant to agree to, Noah gave me a rundown of her recent activities through a video call on my phone. "She never stopped attending Blood U, even during the worst of the conflict and right afterward when the new barons took power," he said. A faint clicking carried through the connection alongside his voice as he must have looked through his notes on another device. "And her parents have never openly come out in support of the old barons or against our current ones."

"Which doesn't tell us much." I frowned at my reflection in the mirror, wondering if it'd be silly to bother with a bit of illusionary magic to give my face more of a made-up look. In the past two years, I hadn't worried about maintaining quite as polished an appearance as I'd used to, but Hadley was used to rich, posh Cressida who'd lorded her family's status over anyone from a less powerful family. "Easier not to publicly pick sides. They didn't have any problem providing the reaper families with 'supplies.'"

"True. Although they were paid for those, and we have no proof that they knew what the animals would be used for."

That was fair. Who could have guessed when it was a new magical strategy the reapers had only just developed? I bit my lip. "So, really, she might not know anything at all. And if she does, there's a significant chance she won't want to tell me because she agrees with their plans."

"It's still worth a shot," Noah said with his usual unflappable energy. "You have a more personal connection to her than any of the rest of us. None of the barons really got to know her in school because of the age difference, and I never really talked to her much. You said she hung out with your group a fair bit back in your junior years?"

"Yeah. But I never considered her a full *friend* back then. You know, the way Victory, Sinclair, and I were, we kind of cultivated… hangers-on who'd do favors for us and who we could boss around." I winced at the memory of how superficial and self-centered I'd been back in my teens.

Noah's voice softened a little. "Maybe that puts you in an even better position. If she has any ties to the reapers that she's been keeping quiet about, you can talk to her from the perspective of someone who's had her own ties and decided you were better off going your own way." His smile turned sly. "That approach seemed to work wonders on Emeric."

I rolled my eyes at the Ashgrave scion. "There may have been a few other factors involved there beyond my political stance."

He laughed. "Maybe, but you did get him to come around politically too. I'm definitely not suggesting you seduce her."

"I didn't seduce Emeric either," I grumbled. If anything, it'd been the other way around, at first anyway.

"I know." Noah fell silent for a moment. "Has he been able to keep you company while all this is going on? I know it's got to be tough for you…"

I could hear from the strain that'd entered his voice how tough it was for *him* not to be here with me. I missed Noah too. My smile tightened, but I forced it wider. "I'm getting by. And now that I'm out of health-center quarantine, he's been coming around a lot. He went to go have lunch with his sister, but he'll be back to spend most of the afternoon with me afterward."

"At least I know you've got someone on your side there," Noah said.

I turned fully toward the phone, my chest constricting

with the longing to reach through the screen to touch Noah's face. "I wish you could be here too. I know why you can't be, and I know you would be if it was safe, so that's not a complaint. But I don't want you to think I'm not missing you."

"You'd better be, *mon petit chou-fleur*," Noah replied, his good cheer returning like I'd hoped it would. He sighed. "Maybe we can figure out something… A joint date from afar? I could watch a movie with you via video chat, or we could all have dinner sort-of together."

My next smile came easier. "Yeah, I'd like that." It still felt strange—but in an exhilarating way—that I had not one but two guys who cared this much about me.

My gaze dropped to the time displayed on the phone, and I made a face. "I'm supposed to meet Hadley in five minutes, so I'd better get going. I'll be in touch right away if I find out anything from her."

"Good luck." Noah reached his hand toward the screen as if he could make contact that way. "I love you."

My heart fluttered in the strange way it always did when he said those words, one I was slowly becoming used to. "I love you too."

After I'd ended the call, I peered at my reflection again and decided to go as I was. My hair was smoothed back into the French braided style I was most comfortable with, new purple and blue streaks added over the past couple of weeks since I'd gotten back home. My blouse and slacks were all professional cool. I didn't want to intimidate Hadley but to encourage her into spilling her guts.

Hopefully something in those guts would be useful to us.

Dragging in a breath, I headed down to the third-floor dorm where Hadley was staying. She'd said a few of her roommates had arrived for the fall term so far, but that they should be out right now so we could talk privately. I had no idea if she had any clue what I wanted to talk to her about… If she knew anything about what the reapers were up to, I'd guess so.

When I rapped on the door, it took what felt like a full minute before Hadley opened it. She swung it wide but then stood there in front of the doorway taking me in rather than motioning me inside.

I took the moment to study her in turn. She didn't look all that different than she had three years ago when we'd last shared a dorm. She still had streaks of turquoise and blue woven into her dark brown hair, a style I'd always suspected she'd modelled after my own creative hair enhancements. Her nose still turned up a bit at the end with its ski-jump curve in a way that made her nostrils look pinched. She was wearing a summer dress that showed off her hourglass curves, the only part of her appearance I'd ever mildly envied.

The critical narrowing of her eyes was new, though. I couldn't remember her ever aiming an expression like that at me while we'd lived together.

"Hey," I said, keeping up my casual cool as well as I could. "Can I come in?"

"Right, of course." Hadley let out a little laugh and stepped to the side to make way.

The dorm common rooms were all laid out pretty much the same, so hers was a close match for mine upstairs. I could spot a few signs of habitation—a hat left on the dining table, a couple of notes tacked to the fridge—but like she'd said, no one else was around. I sank down on one end of the sofa automatically, and Hadley sat across from me. She clasped her hands together in her lap, not tightly but in a gesture I recognized as a nervous one. The tiniest quiver of fear darted from her into the stores of magical energy behind my breastbone.

What *did* she think I'd come about? I really hadn't been all that nice to her back when we'd hung out together much more.

"It's been a while since we really talked," I said in an awkward attempt to break the ice. "Crazy times."

Hadley shrugged. "It's no big deal. I was a little surprised to hear from you."

"Well, there's…" I trailed off, and decided trying to fake small talk would only draw out the awkwardness. "To be honest, I need to ask you about something. I heard the barons already came by and talked to you a few weeks ago."

Her posture stiffened just a tad. "Yes. They asked some questions about you. I'm still not sure what—how they figured I could have been involved—they didn't *accuse* me of anything."

I held up my hands. "And I don't think you should be accused of anything. I know you didn't have anything to do with how I was taken. But… it's turned out there's more to the situation than we realized at first. And it might be related to business your family's been doing with some of the families who call themselves reapers. *I'm* not going to accuse you of any kind of crime either—I'm just hoping you might have seen or heard something that could help me."

"I don't know what I could tell you that would help," Hadley said. "It's my parents' company—I pitch in a little if I'm home and they need something done quickly, but I'm barely involved at all."

"I totally understand that. I was just thinking that if they'd commented at all about the requests from the reaper families—I mean, it would have been pretty unusual, them wanting so many animals. It wouldn't be surprising if your parents remarked on that." If Hadley had *really* been a friend, I'd have asked her if she'd prod her parents for new information, but I could already tell she didn't trust me enough to go that far.

Hadley exhaled in a rush. "I can't remember them saying anything," she said, a little too quickly for me to believe her. She just didn't want to talk about it or maybe even think about it. Who knew how much she might want to stay on the good side of the reaper families in case the tide turned—or how much her parents might already be allied with them?

I groped for the right words. "Look, Hadley… I know I didn't always treat you very well back when we were dormmates. I'm sorry about that. I've had to do a lot of re-evaluating in the last couple of years, as I guess just about everyone knows, with my family situation. Understanding what the reapers were up to with those animals could make a life-or-death difference to me. I'm just trying to survive here."

Hadley opened her mouth and then closed it again. In her hesitation, I pushed a little harder. "It doesn't have to be anything that *sounds* like it'd be super important. But if any of the families who bought those animals mentioned specific criteria they needed in the ones they purchased, or asked questions about their health or behavior, or really anything at all beyond just, 'Give us some cats,' or whatever, it could literally save my life."

And a whole lot of other lives too, but I wasn't sure if that would be laying it on too thick. Would Hadley even believe that Cressida Warbury cared much about people other than herself?

Hadley's gaze flicked to the side and then back to me, and there was a moment when I could have sworn she was going to tell me something. But either my insightful instincts were off, which wasn't impossible, or she changed her mind. Instead, she shook her head. Another faint tickle of anxiety reached me.

"I really didn't hear any details about all that," she said. "If it's important to the barons, I'm sure *they* can go talk to my parents again about it."

They could, and I'd imagine they already were. Noah would have tipped off his brother and colleagues about his discovery too. But my connection to Hadley was the closest thing we'd had to a personal link.

I searched my mind for any observation I'd made of her in the past that might give me a leg up in convincing her, but I came up blank.

Before I could try again, Hadley stood up. "Well, since it seems like I can't help you at all…"

I knew a dismissal when I heard one. I got to my feet, but I couldn't stop myself from making one last attempt, even though embarrassment burned in my chest as the pleading words fell from my mouth. "Please. If you *do* hear anything, or you remember anything… All I've ever done is make the choices that felt right to me, mostly for my survival, even before right now. I've been trying to make those better choices. I just want a chance to live my life without them controlling it."

Hadley's expression only shuttered more. "I'll keep that in mind," she said flatly.

Without any cards I could think of left to play, I trudged out of her dorm and up the stairs to my own. Not even the thought of seeing Emeric soon lifted my spirits. I'd had a chance, and I'd swear she was holding something back, but I hadn't managed to drag it out of her.

For all I knew whatever Hadley had kept to herself wouldn't have solved my problem anyway. That might have been too much to hope for.

As I came out of the stairwell into the fifth-floor landing, my gaze snagged on a startlingly familiar figure standing outside my dorm room. My feet jarred to a halt.

Victory Blighthaven swiveled with a toss of her auburn hair over her shoulder. A smile stretched across her perfectly made-up face. "Cressida! There you are." She folded her arms over her chest. "I heard what happened and figured you could use some moral support so… here I am!"

5

*Emeric*

Shauna picked at her salad, pushing the shreds of lettuce back and forth with her fork. I'd picked up our lunch from the junior cafeteria downstairs, since it didn't seem wise to leave the protection of campus when my former associates were out for my blood. While the school's food wasn't *bad*, I could admit it wasn't the most spectacular meal either. But I didn't think that was the only thing affecting my little sister's appetite.

"I'm sorry," I said, for what was probably the hundredth time in the past two weeks. "I know it sucks that I've asked you to stay on campus. Your friends are probably going into town or wherever all the time—"

"It's fine," she said abruptly. She speared a couple of chunks of vegetables and started chewing them furiously.

I studied her from across the pine table in the small apartment the school headmistress had offered me for my stay here. Nothing in this place was really *mine* except for a few boxes of belongings I'd been able to scavenge from the mess the reapers had left of our house back in Portland. I only had a couple thousand dollars to my name in my bank account. I couldn't do much of anything for my sister that didn't rely on the Blood U staff's generosity.

I tried to take a bite of my BLT, but the mix of bread, veggies, and crisp bacon turned to ash in my mouth. I forced myself to swallow it anyway. Shauna kept her gaze low, swiping a few stray strands of her pale hair back behind her ear.

What could I say to her that I hadn't already? Well, maybe there were a lot of things. I hadn't known what to tell her when I'd gotten back here, half-starved after my, Cressida, and Noah's desperate trek through the Maine wilderness. Shauna knew I'd gotten in deeper with the local reaper families and that my attempt at improving our family's position through that alliance had backfired spectacularly. She knew I felt like shit about it.

But that didn't feel like enough.

"You'd tell me if you've been getting harassed at all, right?" I said, remembering how Cressida's family had managed to send awful messages to her in the hands of students they'd manipulated.

"Everything's fine," Shauna said firmly. Then she sighed and leaned back in her chair. She peeked at me hesitantly through her wispy bangs. "Why are you even doing this?"

I stared at her. "Doing what?"

"Acting like we're this super-close family looking out for each other. You didn't ask hardly anything about how I was doing at school before all this stuff happened."

I opened my mouth and hesitated. I guessed what she'd said was true. Before, I hadn't wanted to talk about the fact that I was letting her go off under the rule of the barons I'd wrongly assumed were traitors, because her learning to use her magic effectively was more important. Maybe I'd been worried that she'd be angry at me for putting her in that position. Maybe I'd wanted to pretend it wasn't happening at all.

Now, I had trouble figuring out where exactly my head had been at when I'd made those decisions.

"I always cared," I said carefully. "I always *wanted* to look out for you. That's why I made sure you enrolled so you could get your education, even though back then I didn't trust the current barons."

Shauna shrugged. "I just mean that you didn't really care what I thought about anything back then, so it's a little weird that you do now."

My stomach knotted. "I'm sorry I made you feel that way. I didn't want you to think you couldn't talk to me, even if I didn't go out of my way to ask."

"Well, it—it was hard. Harder then than it is now." Her jaw tightened for a second, and I realized with a jolt that she was fighting tears. "You were always talking about how the new barons needed to be overthrown, how things would have to change soon, and I—"

She stopped, sounding a little choked. I scooted my chair around the table so I could grasp her arm.

"You what?" I said as gently as I could. "I'm so sorry I wasn't listening then, but I am now. I want to know what you're thinking and feeling."

She sucked in a breath. "I like it here. I always liked it here. And when the barons came around, they never seemed so terrible. But I didn't know how to tell you that. You were so sure… You didn't seem to want to know what I'd seen."

Guilt wrapped tight around my heart. I couldn't argue with her description. I knew how true it'd been. I hadn't wanted to hear Cressida's stories of how the new barons had helped her either.

I closed my eyes, inhaled slowly, and caught Shauna's eyes again. "I know I've said it already, but I really am sorry. For that too. I should never have made you feel that way, and I hate that it took me so long to get my head on straight. But that was my issue, my insecurities, nothing to do with how I feel about you. You're my little sister. You're the only real family I've still got. I want to do a better job now, and that's why I've been asking you to have these lunches and stuff. But if you need some space for a little while before you'd want to spend much time with me—"

Shauna shook her head with a jerk. A couple of the tears she'd been fending off slipped down her cheeks. "No. I—I felt really alone a lot of times since I started coming here. I was just a little afraid to tell you, even now… You're really not mad at me?"

"No, not at all."

I opened my arms and she leaned in for a quick but emphatic hug. When she pulled away, she managed to smile at me. I smiled back even as I kicked myself mentally. There were so many important parts of my life, so many important people, that I'd almost screwed up.

I still might have completely screwed Cressida over.

That last thought lingered in the back of my head through the rest of the lunch. I walked with Shauna out to the green and parted ways with her to veer toward Ashgrave Hall. Cressida was expecting me.

I wasn't totally sure what to say to her either. Every time I thought about the way she'd gone into that unnerving autopilot state in the grip of the reapers' spell, my chest clenched up with panic. What they meant to do —to kill her horribly in their pursuit of revenge against the new barons… How had I *ever* allied myself with those people?

But I had, and now the woman I'd fallen for was paying for it.

I reached her floor of the building and found her standing in her dorm's doorway, talking with a girl I recognized immediately even though I'd been too old to share any classes with her. The Blighthavens were one of the most prominent families outside the baronies, and everyone noticed when one or another was around.

When Cressida flashed me a smile of welcome, Victory looked me over. My skin prickled with an impression of her disdain, but I couldn't tell how much of that was in my head vs. something she'd actually expressed. I'd gotten out of the habit of wearing gloves to hide my titanium hand and forearm around campus, but I had the abrupt urge to tug one on now.

"I didn't know you were expecting company," Victory said to Cressida with a tilt of her head. "Why don't I come by tomorrow and bring brunch, if you won't be busy then?"

Cressida chuckled. "I think my schedule's pretty open. I can fit you in."

Victory sauntered past me with a brief nod my way, and Cressida motioned me into the dorm. I glanced behind me as she closed the door. "What was that about?"

"Oh, just an old friend coming by to see if she can lend a hand," Cressida said. She sounded both pleased and exasperated. "I'm not sure how much Victory can actually *do*, seeing as her family split off from the reapers early on so they don't have any inside info, but at least it's a little more company to keep my mind off of things."

I reached out with my proper hand to brush my fingertips over her cheek. Cressida leaned into my touch, and my heart ached with the stress I saw slipping from her face. I wanted to tell her how much I hated what she was going through and how it killed me not being able to help more myself… but I couldn't dump all my regrets on her when she was already dealing with so much. She didn't even have Noah by her side to lead the way with his baron-ish authority.

I had to be her rock, her certainty in the storm, and keep whatever turmoil was going on inside me as far away from our time together as I could.

"We're going to figure this out," I said. "You've got the entire pentacle of barons on your side, plus all the resources they can draw on. They beat the reapers soundly before, and they'll do it again."

"Well, if even *you* think that highly of their abilities, maybe you're right," she said, managing to take on a playful tone.

I brought my titanium hand to the other side of her face, cupping it. Reveling in the knowledge that she'd never shied away from that part of me. "Mostly I think highly of you."

She tipped forward, and I met her kiss halfway. It was still a new sensation, *getting* to kiss her, especially without any nefarious scheme in the back of my mind. But I couldn't pick up on any hesitation in her. She pressed her mouth to mine wholeheartedly, and I was only too happy to match her passion.

She wanted *me*. She had a soon-to-be baron who adored her, but she still wanted me too. That was nothing short of a miracle.

The heat that raced through me as her lips moved against mine inspired other thoughts about how I could take her mind off her perilous situation. If distraction was the best help I could personally offer, who was I to deny her?

I walked her backward in the direction of her bedroom, dropping my hand to her waist to guide her movements. Our hips brushed against each other, Cressida made a hungry sound low in her throat, and just like that I was hard as titanium in more places than just my hand.

We'd spent the night together yesterday, but it'd been the first night I'd ever spent with just her, so I was still feeling out what she liked and what she'd be comfortable with. I paused for a second when we reached the bedroom, pulling back enough to check her expression, but Cressida just hummed impatiently and tugged on my shirt to bring my mouth back to hers.

That was a clear enough signal. We pushed past her bedroom door, and I eased her down on the bed. The crisp, coolly sweet scent of her filled my nose, and the urge to enjoy her in a way I hadn't gotten to yet swept over me.

As I kissed my way down the side of her neck, I unclasped and unzipped the fly of her slacks. Cressida gasped at the brush of my fingers between her legs. She wriggled free of her pants and outright moaned when I stroked the dampening fabric of her panties.

I claimed her lips again, stroking between her legs until she was squirming against me. Then I charted a path down her body, kissing her throat, her collarbone, the hollow of cleavage showing just above her collar, down over her shirt to the smooth plane of her belly. Cressida's breath caught as she must have realized where I was going.

"You smell amazing," I murmured, pressing another kiss to the hem of her panties. "I can't wait to taste you."

Without a second's hesitation, I tugged her panties down and did just that. I brushed my lips over her mound and slicked my tongue down to her clit. Cressida inhaled sharply, her breath breaking with a moan as I dipped my mouth farther down.

She did taste amazing, tart and musky in the best possible way, her arousal pooling on my tongue. I lapped at her opening and then swiveled my tongue over her clit until she grasped my hair and arched into me with a whimper.

I wasn't exactly a ladies' man, but I'd had my share of lovers. In that time, I'd learned that my false hand was better than my real one in certain special ways. Now, I eased my titanium fingers between Cressida's legs and hooked one right inside her.

Cressida murmured encouragingly, rocking into my touch. I pumped my firm finger in and out, suckling her clit at the same time. When she let out a growl that begged for more, I added a second finger to the mix, and then a third. Stretching her with all that warmed metal, finding the most sensitive places inside her.

I stroked that special spot deep within, and her hips nearly bucked off the bed. Gasping, she clutched my hair even harder.

This I could do. I couldn't fix the horrifying magic embedded in her body, but I could take her out of that body on a wash of pleasure for at least a little while.

I worked my fingers rhythmically inside her, grazing my teeth over her clit at the same moment, and she came with a sweet little cry and a clenching of her walls around my fingers. I smiled against her and caressed her through the last shudders.

I would have stopped there, happy simply knowing I'd gotten her off, but Cressida sat up and pulled me to her. Our mouths crashed together. She showed no sign of minding her taste on my lips, devouring my mouth as she fumbled with the fly of my jeans.

My cock twitched at the brush of her fingers. I helped

her jerk my jeans and boxers down, the throbbing ache of desire winding all along my length.

Cressida wrenched her lips from mine for just long enough to mutter the protective casting over her sex. She splayed her legs around me and arched to meet me, and I slid into her slick heat with a groan.

It was just as much bliss as it'd been that first night what felt like a year ago even though it'd only been a couple of days. I thrust at a steady rhythm, gradually building speed and sinking deeper inside her.

Cressida raised herself up to meet me. I gripped her ass to put her at an even better angle for her own pleasure, and she tipped her head back into the pillow with another moan. She looked so fucking sexy with wisps of her ice-blond hair coming free from her braid around her face and her cheeks flushed with pleasure.

She deserved everything I could offer her. She deserved so much better than the way her asshole family and the other reapers had treated her.

I had the impulse to make her come and come again until I'd sated every possible shred of desire in her, but she squeezed her thighs around my hips and met my gaze, her breath stuttering around her words. "So close. Come with me."

I couldn't have refused her if I'd wanted to. The sultry words shot straight to my cock, and it was all I could do to hold on until she started to shake with her second orgasm. The second her channel clamped around my erection, I came too, with a searing wash of pleasure that blanked out my mind for several seconds.

Cressida hummed contentedly and pulled me down beside her on the bed. I slid my arms around her, and she tucked herself against me as if she'd never been meant to fit anywhere else. Just for a moment, the stresses of her current situation had melted from her body.

Now if only I could actually solve her problem instead of just distracting her from it.

6

*Cressida*

Victory had never really been the picnic type, but I guessed she liked the idea of hanging around near my newly arriving dormmates even less. She marched me down to the field around back of Ashgrave Hall, shot imperious stares at the few students hanging around as if daring them to come any closer, and picked a spot near the edge of the forest where there wasn't anyone around. With a murmur and a quick gesture, she turned a stretch of grass into a woven blanket of sorts.

Persuasion might be her specialty, but she was no slouch at physicality.

Percy soared by in the sky overhead. I glanced up at him with a mental wave of acknowledgment, and he sent me a twinge of happiness at seeing me outside. Maybe I'd been neglecting my familiar a little since all this had started.

I sank onto the blanket across from Victory as she got to work unpacking the bag of brunch treats she'd brought from, I assumed, her family's chef. Between school busy-ness and then the mission that had taken up my time since last term, I hadn't seen my best friend in a few months. She'd been off living her adult life once she'd graduated.

I wasn't totally sure she even did still consider me her best friend. Had we ever known each other *that* well? After the turmoil of the past several weeks, the dark secrets I'd dredged up for Noah and Emeric and the hidden vulnerabilities they'd revealed to me in return, the friendship I'd had with Victory felt much more superficial.

But even when she'd been kind of a bitch in general, she'd always stuck with me. We'd had each other's backs, especially after I'd fallen into disgrace and her family was still as respected as it'd always been, and that counted for a lot. I didn't think she could break the spell that'd upended my life, but having her here gave me a weird sense of security all the same.

"So," she said, handing me a covered plate heaped with French toast, mini quiches, and smoked fish, "your parents really screwed you over this time, didn't they?"

Despite the truth of those words, my lips twitched with a smile at the blunt way she'd stated it. "Yeah, they really have. I guess they figure it's payback for me theoretically screwing them over by changing sides."

Victory rolled her eyes. "Right, because the old barons would totally have won the battle if a single additional mage had fought on their side." She shook off her sarcasm. "So, what are you doing about it?"

Typical Victory, focusing straight on getting to action. I blew out my breath and considered my answer while I chewed a bite of syrupy sweetness. The French toast wasn't quite on the level of the eclairs Noah liked to present me with, but it was damn good all the same.

"There hasn't been a whole lot for me *to* do," I admitted. "It's mostly the doctors and everyone else scrambling to try to figure out this spell—which is all persuasion and physicality, so I don't have any expert knowledge there. There is one person here who might know something useful… You remember Hadley from our junior dorm? But I tried talking to her yesterday, right before you came by, and got nowhere."

Victory hummed to herself. "I don't recall her having the stiffest spine out there. You really couldn't loosen her lips?"

"I made it clear that I wasn't going to accuse her of actively helping the reapers or anything like that. Tried to appeal to her sense of justice, however much she has of that. In the end I practically begged her to take pity on me. No dice."

Victory raised her eyebrows. "Pity? Oh, Cress, have you really forgotten how this works?"

I hesitated. "What do you mean?"

She motioned to the food. "Eat, and we'll keep talking. This whole situation has obviously done a number on you."

I followed her order with a little confusion. It wasn't exactly a trial to keep enjoying the brunch. Victory popped the last bite of a quiche into her mouth and daintily licked her fingertips before leaning back on her hands.

"We were some kind of cunts the first few years we were going to school here, weren't we?"

I couldn't hold back a snort. "That's one way of putting it."

"And maybe we were harder on some of the wrong people than we should have been, and we had our opinions skewed by the stupid things some people want to believe about who's worthy or whatever… but we got things done, didn't we?"

I grimaced at her. "Mostly hurtful things. I'm not proud of a lot of the crap I did."

"Well, neither am I," Victory said with a crooked smile. "But I'm not letting myself be ashamed of it either. I was wrong about some things, and then I figured out what was more right, and I grew from there. We were teenagers. We couldn't be expected to have everything straight in our heads already."

I took another bite of French toast. "Where are you going with this?"

"First, that you shouldn't beat yourself up for what happened years ago. And second…" Victory paused. "You know the kind of work I do."

"I have a vague idea," I said. "You got in with one of the new fearmancer entertainment start-ups that's giving mages ways of generating fear without hurting anyone."

"Yeah, mostly I'm using persuasion spells to encourage Nary investors and consumers to get on board. It requires a lot of subtlety because we don't want them expending more financial resources than they comfortably can, or we'll lose them in the long run, but it's kind of fun." She waved her hand vaguely as if it was no big deal. "Anyway, I was working with this guy ten years older than me who figured that his age meant he was my boss even though we were on the same level."

I could tell his attitude wouldn't have led him anywhere good without even hearing the rest of the story. "What did you do?"

Victory's lips curved into a smirk. "I waited until he screwed up, and then I made a big—but not obviously staged—show of discovering his mistake in front of a couple of the higher-ups. And afterward I had a few... select words with him, but made it clear that if he let me handle my business, I didn't have to be his enemy."

I had to laugh. "Basically the same thing you'd have done with someone pissing you off in class a few years ago."

Victory shrugged. "If it works... That's my point. I didn't really do anything wrong. *He* was wrong, trying to act like he could boss me around, and I showed him who was the real boss without sabotaging him or lying, just using what was there to my advantage. There's nothing wrong with *that*. Even if you're not going to be outright mean, you can still tap into your inner bitch."

I rubbed my mouth. "And I'm guessing this is going to relate to Hadley."

"Of course. She cowered before us back then. We intimidated her. You can pull out the bitch and put her in her place, remind her of how lucky she is to have you giving her the time of day at all, and a switch will flick. That's what people like her respond to."

She might be right, but the thought of going all mean girl on Hadley made my stomach twist. I didn't really want to admit that to Victory and sound like a wimp.

"I've never been as good at the intimidation stuff as you," I pointed out instead. "You were always the one who *really* got things done." Sinclair and I had been happy to ride on Victory's coattails, and obviously we'd packed enough of a punch that Victory had been happy to keep us as her closest confidants, but I wasn't going to kid myself that I could ever have wielded the same kind of social power she had.

Victory shook her head at me. "You can't think that way. You didn't have to be as good at it as me because I was there. I'm not anymore. I think you can step up. It's in there somewhere, or I wouldn't have trusted you enough to hang out with you the way we did. I know the last couple of years have shaken you up a lot, but you can't forget who you are."

She gave me a warmer smile, and a little of the tightness wound up inside me released. I still wasn't sure I wanted to take her advice with Hadley—or that I even could—but it meant something that she'd come by to give me that advice anyway.

"Okay," I said. "Duly noted. Now what else do you have in that bag of wonderful food?"

Victory chuckled and reached into the cloth sack. She was just pulling out another container when a prickling sensation ran through the left side of my gums. I stiffened automatically.

It was nothing. It had to be nothing. There was no way the barons would have risked coming onto campus all together—unless they were trying another test…?

The thought hadn't quite crossed my mind when a sharper pain lanced from that one tooth right down my jaw. I gasped, clamping my hand to the side of my face. At the same moment, the urge to get up and walk back toward the center of campus spread through my limbs.

The exercises—all the practice I'd done with Professor Burnbuck. I focused my mind on the strategies we'd worked out, willing away all thought of the possibility that any negative spell was affecting me. I didn't feel any inclination to walk anywhere at all. I was just sitting here enjoying a nice brunch.

Of course, I couldn't totally keep that illusion up to begin with. A quiver of concerned distress rippled from Percy into me. And Victory was staring at me.

"Cressida—" she started.

"Go to—go to the health center," I said. "Tell them the spell's acting up again. Maybe let the headmistress know too. I should be able to keep myself here out of the way for at least a little while."

I had to let in some awareness of the impulses racing through me to get those words out. My consciousness of the spell's effect wore down my self-control. My legs lurched me onto my feet.

I fixed my gaze on the trees across from me, filling my mind with thoughts of their piney scent and the textures of the shadows between the trunks. Tuning out even my familiar's reaction. Some small part of me noticed Victory dashing off. I didn't let myself think about what she was doing or why she'd be in such a hurry.

The pain dug deeper, all the way around my chin, and it occurred to me that we'd forgotten to account for that factor in our experiments. I'd been tuning out compulsions but not physical discomfort at the same time.

Well, I could deal with the pain head on, since it wasn't forcing me to do anything, just being freaking annoying. As long as I didn't think about *why* it was happening…

I mumbled a casting to send a numbing chill over my jaw. It took the edge off the jabs but didn't erase the pain completely.

Taking slow, even breaths, I trained even more attention on the trees and the whisper of the breeze over my cheeks and hair. On the chirping of a bird hopping from one branch to another. That was all I noticed. I definitely wasn't experiencing any other sensations.

I had no sense of time, because it would have been acknowledging the compulsion to check how long I'd been resisting it. All I knew was that my legs were aching almost as much as my jaw by the time my usual doctor and a few of the other health center staff reached me. They murmured casting words as they came, and a magical barrier formed around my body. I relaxed just a little, my legs jarring against the invisible wall.

They were fighting the compulsion for me now.

"What's going on?" the doctor demanded, frowning as her gaze swept over me. "What set it off?"

She didn't know? "I—I'm not sure," I said. "I assumed it had to be because of the barons…"

I trailed off as she shook her head. "None of them are on campus—even the two scions left for a meeting. Where was it encouraging you to go?"

"I couldn't tell. Just—toward the buildings and the green." I paused and let myself pay more attention to the urge gripping me now that I safely could. No details came with the impressions that shivered through me, only the increasingly frantic sense that I needed to head back… to Ashgrave Hall? To Nightwood Tower? To a specific person?

Nothing definite presented itself. My heart sank with the one clear conclusion I could draw.

There was more to the spell than we knew—or else the reapers had managed to change how it'd be provoked without ever coming near me.

I'd never know for sure whether I was safe, no matter how vigilantly I kept away from the people I cared about.

7

*Cressida*

Pain splintered through my gums. It was only an illusion, but it sure *felt* real enough to make me wince.

Professor Razeden spoke his persuasive casting, his voice so low I couldn't really hear what he'd ordered me to do. But my body responded anyway, as planned. My knees wobbled with the urge to sit, and I had to catch myself before I crumpled, forcing my legs straight again.

I caught my breath and returned to the tried-and-true strategy of pretending nothing was directing me at all. This time, I actually embraced the pain, letting the jabs of it overwhelm every other thought.

It wasn't a *pleasant* distraction, but it was effective. And leaning into the thing the reapers meant to use to force my hand as a way of defeating their influence instead made me weirdly happy.

I was used to pain. I'd gone through plenty at both my parents' hands and others' over the years. I could tolerate it knowing that it was shielding me from something worse—from doing damage to who knew how many innocent people.

We had no idea what the reapers' new goal for me was, what they'd hoped to accomplish with that last call to my spell, but I didn't intend to give them the chance to show us.

My whole head was throbbing by the time the persuasive casting finally overcame my will and my legs bowed. I sank into the floor with a muttered curse.

The pain vanished in an instant as Professor Burnbuck dispelled the illusion. "That was excellent," he said, sounding genuinely impressed. Who would have thought I'd find my greatest strength in preventing myself from exploding?

I guessed I couldn't deny that avoiding that fate was excellent motivation.

I let out a huff of frustration and flopped back on the cool floor of the desensitization chamber. The curved black ceiling glowered down at me. The professors exchanged a few words, and Razeden left. Burnbuck must have figured I'd had enough. He wasn't wrong.

Too bad the reapers weren't giving me the same consideration.

The professor walked over to stand within my view, peering down at me. "You really shouldn't be disappointed in your performance. You're keeping better control every time we practice, and you held yourself together admirably when the spell gripped you without warning yesterday."

I grimaced. "It's hard to know exactly what I'll need to do in the future when I don't know what they're after now, though, isn't it? It's not enough just to keep me apart from the barons."

"I would suspect, as the health center staff have already concluded, that the reapers were simply attempting to direct you off campus where they could take you back into… custody," Burnbuck said. "As long as you can delay the effect long enough to get help, you'll be fine."

"Until they switch tactics again." I sat up and rubbed my forehead. I'd spent all yesterday afternoon and the whole night in the health center's shielded room. The tug of the spell had eased off after an hour or so, but its absence hadn't comforted me. I kept bracing for it to come back.

"It doesn't feel like enough," I added. "They have all this control over me, and all I can do is temporarily fend them off until someone else can come save me. I wish there was a way I could actually work toward *stopping* them."

Burnbuck's mouth twisted with sympathy. "I can understand you feeling that way, Cressida. It isn't your fault that you aren't an expert in these specific arts. Even the mages who *are* experts in persuasion and physicality are needing time to pick apart how the spell works."

"I know." But his words triggered something in my head, something that didn't exactly lift my hopes but at least stirred them a little. My gaze slid away from him as I turned the idea over in my mind.

I wasn't an expert on any kind of magic, not really. Even with my greatest strength—illusions—it would take years more of experience to get to that level of proficiency. But there were other things I was a sort of expert on. Noah had asked me to talk to Hadley because of my personal connection to her, relatively slim as that was.

What about my family and the friends they'd had around throughout my childhood? If I was an expert in *anything*, it should be the Warbury family. I might not be aware of the details of a lot of their businesses and other activities, but I should know more than anyone who wasn't currently allied with the reapers.

I couldn't exactly go to them and badger them for information, but what if I could connect information I could get here to things I already knew about them?

I sat up a little straighter. "I can't go to the teachers' wing in Killbrook Hall, right? Because Noah and Agnes are staying there?"

Professor Burnbuck nodded. "That's the current ruling of the health center staff, and given recent developments, it seems particularly wise to remain cautious."

"Yeah. I was just thinking— Professor Viceport has been helping with studying the spell." I'd seen the physicality professor a few times while the team working on my case had examined me. "Do you think she'd meet me somewhere else so I could talk with her? I'd like to get a better understanding of how the physical part of the spell works."

Burnbuck eyed me curiously, but he didn't argue with my request. "I can speak to her. I'd imagine she'd be willing to join you in the library, if that works. I can have her text you the exact time she'll be available."

I let out my breath with a tiny sense of relief. "That would be perfect. Thank you."

Professor Viceport was very prompt, maybe because she saw the situation as particularly urgent. She arrived at the library just a minute after I'd gotten there and ushered me over to a table in a private corner. Classes had just started today, but not many students were already hitting the books.

Viceport sat down across from me and folded her hands on the tabletop. She had a cool, elegant poise I'd always admired, her icy blue eyes considering me from behind her rectangular glasses, her slim frame drawn up perfectly straight. She tipped her head to me. "Miss Warbury. Professor Burnbuck indicated that you wanted to speak to me about our progress in studying the spell that's been placed on you."

I nodded. "I was just thinking… if I understood it better, maybe I could figure out something that would help us find a solution or at least point us in the right direction. When I was growing up, I got to know and hear a lot about the families my parents associate with. I might make a connection that'd be useful."

"A reasonable hope," Viceport said. "As you can

probably guess, my knowledge is mostly focused on the physicality side."

"Of course. It seemed like that's the side that would involve more active experimenting or whatever. I mean, persuasion is pretty straightforward. Other than determining what they want to persuade me to do, which the spell isn't necessarily going to tell me if they can change their minds without warning."

A little bitterness might have crept into my tone. Viceport gave me a sharp look. "We *will* overcome the problem you're facing. You have some of the finest minds in fearmancer society working on it, and it affects not just you but all of us, as I doubt the reaper contingent will stop using their new technique after just a couple of iterations. We're very invested in finding answers quickly."

I'd been so wrapped up in how the spell affected me and those immediately around me that I hadn't considered the broader implications—all the other ways the reapers might use this kind of strategy. A chill washed over my skin. "Right. I guess it's just hard not to be worried that I'm going to be a casualty on the way to getting to those answers. Which wouldn't be your fault. It would just suck for me."

Viceport's tone turned a bit wry. "Yes, I can imagine it would. I appreciate your interest in helping, however selfish those motives may be. I think with your life on the line, you have more than enough reason to think about yourself first anyway."

I leaned forward, spurred on by her acceptance of my quest. "So, what do you know about the physicality aspect of the spell so far? I realize there's an explosive component… I guess that's tied to some kind of trigger. Being close to enough of the barons all at once must be one of the triggers, if not the only one."

"Yes, we have to assume that much based on the behavior the persuasive aspect has driven previously. We've also caught small amounts of essence from the barons' family lines tangled into the spell." Viceport paused. "We suspect they'll have reached out to the remaining parents of those barons, the ones who'd have cooperated—Baron Nightwood's mother, Baron Stormhurst's father. We're not sure how they included the other aspects, but it could require no more than a hair or a bit of skin."

"And it seems like a major factor is how well they kept all of the energy shielded inside… inside my tooth, in this case, so that no outside spells could detect it before it activated," I said.

"Yes, I'll admit that's the part that's caused us the most difficulty." Viceport's gaze went distant as she pondered the situation for a moment. "I know Noah Ashgrave has come across evidence that points to the use of test subject animals. It would definitely be necessary to try out this kind of spell on multiple living hosts to perfect it. But the persuasive aspect would be the trickiest aspect there—I know that much. Not many mages can compel a being that doesn't understand the language they're using."

My pulse stuttered. I should have thought of that aspect before. "My parents were friends with a couple— the husband was particularly good with animals. He used to brag about how he could frighten Naries by making their pets turn on them." I shuddered at the memory of his triumphant tone. "That was the… the… Hairrots. I don't remember their first names."

Viceport didn't perk up as much as I'd hoped she would at my brainstorm. "The blacksuits and in some cases the barons themselves have questioned your parents and all their known associates," she said. "They haven't been able to lay charges against anyone except the families in Portland who were most directly responsible for your kidnapping. The other families were able to claim that they had no idea what was going on. I know they were all looked at closely for suspicious activity both then and when everyone was searching for you. I don't think there's anything public that we can turn up."

There might be something private, though. We'd visited the Hairrots' country estate a few times—they kept a small farm, partly because the husband had liked having the animals around to work his skills on, I suspected, not that he'd admitted it. It'd had a lot of room and was very private. Had the reapers run their experiments there?

But the blacksuits couldn't justify searching it only on my suspicions based on conversations years ago that hadn't been tied to the current situation at all. If *I* went out there and took a look around…

The thought of stepping beyond the campus wards made my skin tighten up. It was hard enough resisting the spell while I was here. Would it hit me even harder out there? Even if it didn't, the reapers might be waiting for any chance they could take to wipe me out completely.

I dragged in a breath. "Is there anything significant

about the physicality aspect—something that stands out as unusual?"

Viceport cocked her head. "The treatment of your tooth itself is quite a feat. They've essentially turned it into a conducting device, but only on the inside with just a tiny opening near the base between the teeth here no one would notice if they weren't searching. To create such a precise and delicate hollow without disturbing the nerves in any way would require more skill than I can say I could bring to it."

Which of my parents' friends had done any major work with conducting devices? I strained my mind, and a vague memory came back to me—a piece Mom had kept at our smaller cottage property, one she'd said she'd gotten from a friend, that cooled or heated whatever room it was in to the preferences of the person holding it. I couldn't remember what the friend's name was, but it'd been painted on the bottom of the piece in neat little letters that hadn't stuck in my mind.

That conducting piece was far beyond the secure boundaries of Blood U too.

Viceport offered me a regretful smile. "I'm sorry. I can't think of anything else particularly noteworthy about the spell other than how precisely and uniquely it combines all those elements, which you already knew. If the information leads you down any interesting paths, let me or anyone else on staff know."

"I will," I said, and watched her leave with a twist in my gut.

How far was I going to go to get answers? How far was

it even worth going? I couldn't help anyone if some reaper burnt out my brain within five minutes of me leaving campus.

I looked down at my hands, grappling with my nerves, and my mind drifted to my conversation with Victory yesterday.

She would have told me to suck it up and ignore my fears. But she'd also pointed out that I hadn't really exhausted all my options when it came to the avenues of investigation I had right here on campus.

Before I stuck my neck out even farther, maybe I should give being a bitch a try.

8

*Cressida*

Before confronting Hadley this time, I did cast a glamour illusion over my face. If I was going to channel my old mean-girl self, I figured I'd better look the part.

I kept my eyes trained on my reflection in the mirror as I murmured one casting word and then another, carefully darkening the rims of my eyes, thickening and lengthening my eyelashes, smoothing out a few minor blemishes on my skin, and adding a rosy glow to my pale cheeks. I finished by touching up my lips to a deeper shade of pink. When I was done, I was as artfully made-up as any movie star, although it was all an illusion. At least that made taking the "make-up" off a lot easier when I wanted to. I could dispel it with a snap of my fingers.

Emeric stood up from where he'd been watching from the edge of my bed and came over. Stopping behind me, he slipped his arms around me and studied me from over my shoulder.

"Very impressive work," he said. "But then, I always think you look impressive."

I let out a skeptical sound even as I sank into his embrace. His company was the one comfort I still had right now, and I was going to make the most of it. "As my boyfriend, I'm pretty sure it's your job to say that."

He chuckled. "Doesn't mean I don't mean it." He pressed a kiss to the crook of my jaw and then caught my eyes in the mirror again, his turning a little more serious. "So, is it official then?" he said, in a tone that sounded carefully light. "I'm your boyfriend?"

The uncertainty he was trying to cover up sent a pang through my heart. He'd been with me as much as he could over the past few days, supporting me more than I suspected many spouses even would have, but I couldn't blame him for not being sure. The day the reapers' spell had first activated, I'd only just told him I was interested in him in a romantic way—again, after all the turmoil we'd been through before. We hadn't really talked about our relationship status since.

"I think that's the only reasonable word for a guy who's been taking care of me so well in so many ways," I said, matching his tone and adding a teasing lilt. "Just as long as you still have no objections to not being my *only* boyfriend…"

Emeric full-out laughed. "It might be a little more… interesting navigating that when Noah can be in the picture more again, but so far I haven't had any second thoughts." He hugged me a little tighter. "And I'm glad I could be here for you now, especially when he can't be."

I swallowed hard. "I'm glad too." And I would have shown him just how glad if I didn't know because of Noah's sleuthing that Hadley was due to leave her class in Nightwood Tower in less than ten minutes.

I turned in Emeric's arms to give him a lingering kiss, since I did have time for that. As I stepped back, he squeezed my hand before letting me go. "You can handle this. I know how strong—and stubborn—you are."

"We'll see," I said. "My bitch skills are a little out of practice."

I got into the zone as well as I could on my way down the stairs, pulling my shoulders back and my posture straight, raising my chin at just the right haughty angle to be looking down my nose at anyone who wasn't significantly taller than me. I ran through the potential scenarios I'd imagined, what I'd say if she said or did this thing or that.

Even though taking someone down a peg had come automatically to me just a couple of years ago, my stomach was full of nervous butterflies. I ignored their twitching as well as I could and strode out across the green so I'd be in the right place as soon as Hadley emerged.

As usual, the students came out in an erratic trickle. I stood to the side of the door, watching for the distinctive streaks in her hair. My gaze snagged on her the second she came into view. She was alone, which served my purposes just fine.

I waited until she'd gotten a few steps from the tower and then moved to smoothly intercept her.

"Hey," I said in a confident tone that was channeling Victory more than my old self, and caught Hadley by the arm to steer her even farther from our peers.

Hadley's head jerked around, and she stumbled when she saw who'd grabbed her. A cold shiver of startled fear traveled from her into me. That seemed like a good start.

I kept my grip loose, but when I fixed her with my best icy stare, she didn't pull away. If anything, I could see her expression getting meeker.

Maybe Victory really had been on to something.

"We need to talk," I announced, still guiding her toward the field around the back of the building. "Properly."

"I—talk about what?" Hadley stammered, more little jolts of energy reaching me from her uneasy nerves. "I told you that I haven't heard anything—"

"Well, here's the thing, Hadley." I stopped and immediately swiveled toward her, setting my hands on my hips. My gut clenched at taking on the pose that had been associated with cruelties in my past I wished I could erase, but I wasn't going to hurt her. And I was only badgering her to save not just my life but possibly that of the barons and who knew how many other students as well.

"I think you know more than you're saying," I went on. "Maybe you're scared of the consequences of talking—from the reapers or from the blacksuits. Maybe you're actually on the reapers' side, because sure, who wouldn't want to be ruled by assholes who torment anyone who doesn't agree with them. But either way, I would have hoped you'd have developed a little more guts by now. You'd really just stand by while there are so many lives at stake?"

I let out a little huff and shook my head as if in disappointment. This was one concession I'd made to my current morality—I wasn't going to directly threaten her or belittle her for the kinds of superficial reasons I might have in the past. I could shame her for *her* lack of morality just as easily.

Coming from me with the same approach I'd have used when we were younger, my disdainful attitude appeared to have a similar effect. Hadley winced and stared at me wide-eyed, maybe trying to figure out how the woman who'd begged her a couple of days ago had transformed back into the second-in-command bitch. Or maybe I was the head bitch, now that Victory had graduated. That was a weird thought.

She rallied, though, her own chin coming up with a hint of defiance. "I don't see how you have any right to badger me about it."

I raised my eyebrows. "Oh, no? You do realize that I'm good friends with Baron Bloodstone and dating the soon-to-be second Ashgrave baron, don't you? If they find out you refused to help with a situation this critical when you did know something, let's just say I don't think they'll be very pleased."

I didn't really like playing the card of my connections either, but Hadley's resolve visibly wavered. She sucked her lower lip under her teeth. "There really wasn't anything," she said. "Nothing important."

"Great," I said. "Nothing *important.* Tell me all about the unimportant stuff."

"Well…" She sighed. "My parents thought it was strange because these clients were asking for information on different animals' dental characteristics. Like, their teeth. But that—that isn't a surprise, right?"

She glanced at my mouth. Probably word had spread pretty far about my specific condition by now with so many people working on the situation.

And she was right—that report didn't really help. I folded my arms over my chest. "Anything else? Did you ever see any of the people who came around to pick up the animals, or did your parents mention specific clients?"

Hadley looked like she was squirming inside her skin. Another shudder of fearful energy passed into my chest. "I think they already talked to the barons about that back when you were missing. I'm sure they told them everything they knew."

"And what about what *you* know?" I pressed.

"I—well—"

She cut herself off, with an expression as if she'd thought better of what she was going to say, but I wasn't letting her get away with silence. My old demeanor had become more comfortable the longer I'd had it back on, and I felt almost exhilarated as I narrowed my eyes at her. "Hadley, do you really think you're in any position to play these kinds of games? With *me*? I might have parted ways with my parents, but I was still raised by two fearmancers who're powerful and spiteful enough to do this to their own daughter." I motioned to my offending tooth.

Hadley actually shivered, the trickle of fear she'd been sending to me heightening into a momentary flood. Maybe I'd gone a bit overboard.

But it was hard to have any regrets when the next second she opened her mouth. "It wasn't at my parents' business. I don't know for sure it was involved. But I did hear—sometime last year, I was at a party and I heard Sinclair Shadewick complaining to one of the other girls in class about how she'd gotten scratched by a couple of cats that weren't even smart enough to be familiars. I kind of wondered then why she'd been around those cats at all."

Oh, ho. That *was* something, probably more than Hadley even realized.

Sinclair and I had been Victory's close confidants, but we'd gone in totally different directions during the war between the barons and the scions. The Shadewicks had thrown their lot in with the reapers whole-heartedly, to the point that Sinclair had left Blood U without graduating after their side had lost.

I hadn't spoken to her, hadn't even seen her, since then. But she definitely hadn't been an animal lover. Her familiar was a hedgehog, low maintenance and easy to ignore when she wanted to, and she'd never warmed up to Victory's Siamese cat familiar. I couldn't imagine her playing with a couple of cats for fun or whatever.

She'd also been good with both physicality and persuasion, physicality being her specialty. It wouldn't be surprising for the reapers to have asked her to pitch in with their experiments, would it?

I did my best not to let my sense of triumph show. As if that piece of information wasn't enough, I stepped a little closer to Hadley, employing my loom. "That's it? Are you *absolutely* sure you haven't left anything out?"

She nodded frantically. "Totally. I'm—I'm sorry I didn't say anything before. It just seemed so unlikely to make a difference, and I didn't want to get my parents in trouble by provoking more scrutiny, you know…"

I did understand, but this wasn't the right time to show sympathy. I gave her a dismissive wave of my hand. "Sure, sure. I can't promise the barons won't look into your family's business more, but I suppose I can let them know that you did cooperate at least a little."

"Thank you," she said with an audible swallow, and scurried off like the mouse she was.

I inhaled and exhaled a few times, grounding myself with the cooling September air and the firm, grassy ground beneath my feet. I'd brought out my inner bitch, and it'd worked. It'd even been kind of… fun. I didn't want to look at that fact too closely.

I wasn't ever going to become the girl I'd been back then again. Too many horrible memories were tangled up in that time. That didn't mean I couldn't use those strategies when they'd get a job done that needed doing, just like Victory had said.

A smile playing with my lips, I turned back toward the green, meaning to head back to my dorm and video chat with Noah about the conversation I'd just had. But I'd

only made it two steps when a screeching sound split
the air.

I whipped around just in time to see a wave of
churning, fiery magic tearing across the field toward
Killbrook Hall—and me.

9

*Cressida*

Thankfully, I had pretty decent instincts for self-preservation. At the first sight of the surge of magic, my heart lurched, and then my legs were propelling me toward the relative shelter of Nightwood Tower as fast as they could go.

I threw myself to the ground around the stone side just as the onslaught crashed into both the tower and the hall across from it. A wash of heat flared through the air, singeing my skin, and an acrid smoky scent filled my nose.

The building behind me groaned. For a second, I was afraid the tower was going to come crashing right down on me. But the old bricks held, how much from the strength of the mortar and how much the protective spells laced through its framework, I had no idea.

I glanced over at Killbrook Hall and cringed. The

stonework along the side where the casting had hit it was scorched, blackened tongues licking around the edges.

The grass all across the field I'd been standing on moments ago was blackened too. That was what was giving off the smoky smell. If I hadn't moved as quickly as I had, I might have been charcoal.

What the hell was going on? I'd never seen a magical attack on the school like this, not even when a bunch of the old barons' supporters had stormed the campus in the middle of the conflict between them and their scions. And after that whole war, as far as I knew, the remaining school staff had removed any fearmancer who wasn't currently attending the school or an approved family member of a student from the wards.

No one who wasn't on our side should be able to even properly locate the edges of campus to target the school.

Since the war, Ms. Grimsworth had also increased security. Blacksuits burst from the doors of Killbrook Hall, a few more rushing over from Ashgrave Hall and over by the health center. Several other staff who weren't specifically trained for defense hurried out behind them. They were all shouting to each other and snapping out castings, looking as bewildered as I felt.

Then it came again. Another surge of energy, tearing toward us with a deeper roar this time. The sound raised the hairs on the back of my neck. As I scrambled to my feet, the staff who'd emerged all thrust out their hands and hollered emphatic casting words.

The wave of magical fire that'd been racing toward us

smacked into an invisible wall halfway across the charred field. It flickered and flashed against the transparent surface for a few moments before dwindling away.

I might have been more relieved by the apparent victory if I hadn't seen several of the staff letting out ragged breaths or wiping sweat from their foreheads. The defense had taken a lot out of them. How many more attacks could they shield us from?

The more of us that combined our skills, the stronger we'd be. I headed over to join them, keeping a close watch to make sure I wasn't coming near any of the people I was supposed to be steering clear of. Were any of the barons on campus? Was this a different kind of attack targeting them?

A bunch of other students were hustling out of the various buildings, the younger ones rushing from Nightwood Tower or Killbrook Hall to the relative safety of the far side of campus, the older ones gathering with the staff like I had.

"What's going on?" someone asked. "Who's doing this?"

"We don't know," one of the blacksuits said brusquely. "Our priority for now is keeping all of you safe. Anyone with skill in shielding and diffusing spells is welcome to lend their magic, but please let us take the lead."

I was more than happy to stay in the background. Especially because it looked like our attackers were changing tactics.

Instead of a roar, the next sound that pierced my ears

was more of a needling whine. My skin twitched, and a hail of blazing mini meteors rained down on us from above—still coming from the east.

I wasn't especially talented in either of the areas the blacksuit had mentioned, but I knew enough that I could contribute. I raised my voice alongside the dozens of others, channeling my magic and my sense of the need to form a barrier over us into the construct the staff were already conjuring.

We got it up just in time. A couple of the fiery pieces whipped through at the last second, and blacksuits barked other casting words to douse the flames. The rest pummeled the invisible dome we'd build over our heads and sputtered out.

"Hold your ground here," one of the blacksuits ordered his colleagues. "We're going to see if we can't tackle the mages casting these spells."

A contingent of about ten figures dashed toward the forest in the direction the spells appeared to be coming from. A few had their lips already moving, intoning castings as they went.

I took in the scorched stones of the buildings around me, and my stomach tied itself in one big knot. We might have been able to deflect the later attacks, and the protections already embedded in the buildings had fended off the worst of the first one, but no one should have been able to violate the security of Bloodstone University to begin with.

It had to be the reapers, didn't it? They were pissed off

that their plan to use me as a magical bomb hadn't worked, so they'd decided to blow us up some other way. Had they come up with yet another new spell that'd allowed them to bypass the wards?

I didn't have time to ponder that possibility, because the next second, another shriek rattled my eardrums. Even more students were gathering now, and all our heads jerked this way and that, our stances tensed to take on the next threat.

This time the magical attack was made up of tiny spears of searing light, as if our enemies had hoped they could make the projectiles narrow enough that we wouldn't see them in time. Or maybe there was another purpose. As they struck the barrier we'd already conjured, several managed to pierce right through.

Penetrating the layer of magic slowed them down, giving the staff around us time to sputter out a few new deflective castings. One of the spears still managed to slice across one girl's shoulder. She flinched and snatched at the wound, blood welling up through her fingers.

A teacher grabbed her and hurried her toward the health center. Everyone else called out casting words to strengthen our shields, and I added my voice to theirs.

My heart thumped fast with panicked anticipation. What were they going to throw at us next?

But there was a long period without any activity at all. Then a couple of the blacksuits who'd strode into the woods marched back out. As I watched them, wondering what they'd discovered, the woman glanced at me. The second she'd caught sight of me, she pushed onward twice as quickly, waving to her companion and heading straight toward me.

An uneasy wobble passed through my stomach. I couldn't help glancing behind me in case there was something much more notice-worthy over there that they might actually be focused on. But no, it was only regular students around me—and when I looked back at the blacksuits, their gazes were clearly trained right on me.

"Miss Warbury," the woman said, reaching me a step ahead of her partner. "I'd like you to come with us." She grasped my elbow, leaving no room for argument.

"I—okay." I fell into step beside her, stumbling a bit as she dragged me faster than I'd started walking. "What's going on? Where are we going?"

"We'll discuss the first part further once we're in a secure location. And that requires going to the health center."

Great. Back into the impenetrable room where I'd already spent way too much of the past few days. I would have groaned if I wasn't still so keyed up from the fight.

I checked the gathered staff and students. There still hadn't been another attack. "Is everyone else going to be okay?" I asked. "Did you catch the people who were attacking us?"

"Our colleagues have the situation under control," the man said. "That's none of your concern right now."

Something about his tone raised my hackles. "Of course it's my concern. This is my school too. I have friends here. I don't want to see anyone get hurt."

"The best way to make sure no one gets hurt is to hurry up and come with us," the woman said shortly.

They escorted me the rest of the way to the health center, the woman never loosening her grip on my arm. Percy wheeled in the sky overhead, the sense of my distress having drawn him from the shelter he'd taken in the western woods. I sent him a whiff of reassurance that I couldn't put all my will behind.

I didn't really know if everything was okay, did I?

We wound through the white-walled halls to the room that blocked out any outside spells. Inside, the blacksuits motioned for me to sit in my usual chair. I sank onto the lightly padded leather surface, looking from one to the other of them.

"Are you going to tell me what this is all about? I haven't felt any effects of the spell. Was one of the barons on campus—did they get close without me realizing it?"

The woman sighed. "Well, that answers the first question we were going to ask you. You haven't felt any indication of the spell working on you at all?"

I frowned and shook my head. "No. My tooth hasn't ached, and I haven't felt any compulsion to go anywhere or do anything."

"Have you experienced any other unusual effects?" the man asked.

"Other than flaming projectiles descending from the sky?" I muttered, and smoothed out my tone at their sharp look. "No, nothing about *me*. The only strange things I've seen are the attacks that just got thrown at us. It was the reapers or someone working with them, wasn't it?"

"As far as we can tell." The woman's phone buzzed, and she raised it to her ear. "Yes. Yes, I'm with Miss Warbury now." She paused. "I see. That does confirm our initial impressions. All right."

As she hung up, a chill wrapped around my gut. "You don't think *I* had anything to do with the attack, do you?" I said. "I had no idea it was coming. The first wave nearly fried me." Of course, if they really wanted to accuse me of turning traitor in the opposite direction, they might say I'd only staged that moment to appear innocent.

But the woman's mouth slanted at an unexpectedly sympathetic angle. "No, Miss Warbury, we don't think you consciously aided the attack. Unfortunately, it appears that you may have offered assistance through no will of your own."

The chill turned even icier. For a second, I couldn't breathe. "What are you talking about?"

The man spoke up. "We traced a thread of magic bypassing the wards and stretching into campus. That thread led to you. It's what allowed the attackers—who we'd assume are the reapers, since they should be the only ones who'd know how to identify your spell as a target—to home in on the campus in spite of our protections.

"Oh." I swallowed hard. The pieces started clicking together in my head. "They were using me. The spell they put in me. They had a way of seeking it out." And I'd played the bullseye in their assault on Blood U.

I leaned back in the chair and rubbed my hands over my face. "I had no idea. I honestly didn't feel anything different."

"As soon as we got you into this room, the attacks our colleagues were fending off along the boundaries of campus stopped," the woman said. "The reapers can't trace you in here."

"But I can't stay in this room for the rest of my life!" I burst out, and immediately flushed with embarrassment. "I'm sorry. It's just—it's a lot."

"Of course." The man drew in a breath. "We need to go back and confer with the other blacksuits. We'll have the doctors check you over in case there's any lingering sign of how the attackers targeted you."

They stalked out of the room, leaving me alone and on the verge of hopelessness.

I closed my eyes and opened them again. An ache squeezed my heart. I'd been out there *trying* to help defend the school while I'd actually been the one putting it under threat in yet another way. I was a total liability here.

My thoughts hesitated over that realization. I was a total liability *here*. Because the reapers wanted to strike at the university, which was one of the main centers of loyalist activity. My presence on campus also prevented the barons from taking full advantage of the school's security. I'd been putting everyone at risk from the moment I'd returned here.

So maybe it was time I left.

The reapers had made a whole lot of problems for me, and I'd spent the entire time reacting to each problem as they came up. What Victory had said about tapping into my inner bitch didn't only apply to Hadley. I couldn't sit around waiting for someone else to save me.

No matter how nervous I was about leaving the safety of the wards myself, this place was no longer secure for me —or for anyone else while I was here. So it was time for this mean girl to go on the offensive and tackle the shit that'd been flung at me head on.

10

*Noah*

As Cressida's image appeared on the laptop screen, I shifted restlessly on the wooden seat in the pentacle's main meeting room. It always felt a little wrong to be talking to the woman I loved at a distance, through a screen rather than face to face, but never more so than when I was greeting her along with several colleagues in my official role as baron-to-be.

Cressida peered out at us. I recognized the white walls around her as the isolation room in the health center. We'd gotten a report from the staff about how the reapers appeared to have used Cressida to launch a surprise assault on Bloodstone University yesterday.

She looked like she'd barely slept since then. Every muscle in my body ached with the urge to go to her and hug her, offering whatever comfort I could.

But being Cressida, she drew her posture up straight

and put on her typical show of resilience. "Thank you for speaking with me. The doctors insist that I need your permission before they'll give their approval too."

"Of course," Hector said. "We know you're in an increasingly difficult situation, and if there's some way we can assist while you're taking so many steps to ensure our own safety, we're happy to."

"Okay. Well…" Cressida dragged in a breath. "This might sound crazy, so let me explain a little before you really consider it. I think the best thing for me to do would be to leave Blood U."

The roar of blood rushing past my ears was so sudden and loud it drowned out her next few words, despite her insistence that we keep listening. *No!* every part of me screamed. It was bad enough that I couldn't be with her without her leaving the one safe place she had.

But Cressida was still talking. I managed to gather myself enough to focus on her voice again.

"I know there's a lot of risk," she was saying. "But that risk would pretty much all be for *me*. As long as I'm on campus, I'm still at risk too—and I'm putting everyone else here in danger as well. It's not like I'm going to have much of a life stuck in this room anyway. We could arrange some way for you all to track where I am, maybe using my phone? So that you're never close enough that the spell could be a threat to you. And I'd check in with whatever doctors or experts you want as often as you want."

My heart was still thumping away, but at the same time I couldn't deny that she was making sense. I'd probably have wanted the same thing if I'd been in her position. Still, I couldn't help speaking up. "It might not take that much longer to find a way to counter the reapers' spell. If we just gave it a couple more days, we might be able to fix this without *anyone* being in danger."

Cressida's mouth twisted. I suspected she liked arguing with me less than with anyone else. "It doesn't seem like this problem is going to get fixed that quickly. And the reapers have already shown twice that they can use their casting in ways we hadn't anticipated. What if it turns out even the shielding around this room isn't enough to stop them from tracking it? I don't really want to wait around and find out that I'm not actually safe at all."

My stomach sank. That made sense too. Fuck. I grappled with myself, torn between the desire to support her bid for freedom and my need to know she'd be okay.

I couldn't really know that, no matter where she was, could I? There were no guarantees in the awful position the reapers had put her in. She was making the best she could of a bad situation, and even as I balked, I admired her for that.

Declan tapped the tabletop. "Isn't there some concern about the compulsion in the spell increasing once you're outside the university wards? I know you've made excellent progress in your ability to resist its effects, but if it comes over you even stronger, you may not be prepared. And we can't be sure what the reapers might manipulate you into doing in the wider world."

Cressida nodded. "I understand that concern. I've already talked to the staff here, and they're having a conducting piece constructed for me that should create a similar effect to the school wards, just on a much smaller scale. From what they've said, that'll put me on about the same playing field as when I'm here—for the direct impact on me. It's how my departure could affect the rest of you that they weren't sure of."

"Where would you go?" Rory asked, her eyebrows drawing together. I could tell she wasn't asking only for logistical reasons but because she was genuinely worried about how her friend would get by off-campus. Cut off from her family, Cressida didn't have a real home beyond the dorms right now.

Cressida shrugged. "I have plenty of funds. I figured I'd start with a hotel and maybe find a short-term rental if need be." She paused. "And it isn't just that I want to make sure I'm not a threat to everyone on campus. My parents are obviously very involved in this whole situation, and I must know them and some of their associates better than anyone else on our side. I'm hoping I can do a little… investigating and maybe speed us along toward a permanent solution."

My pulse stuttered all over again. She wasn't just going to leave behind the protections of the school but also put herself directly in our enemies' crosshairs.

I bit back the protest that wanted to leap from my throat. It was her life, and I couldn't blame her for wanting to take control of it. Again, I could easily imagine myself making the same choices in her position. If I spoke up against her, I'd only be undermining her freedom. As much as I wanted to protect her, this wasn't my call to make.

I braced myself and forced out the words. "Cressida's suggestions sound reasonable to me. She's obviously thought through the important factors, and having her help against the reapers could give us the advantage we need to shut down this rebellion."

My gut had clenched while I'd spoken, but Cressida's warm smile of gratitude melted quite a bit of my reservations. I'd done the right thing, even if I hadn't enjoyed doing it.

To my relief, the expressions around the table looked accepting. Hector leaned forward. "We will want to sort out a tracking method to ensure we can keep a careful distance from you. But otherwise, as far as I'm concerned, your proposal is fair."

His words about keeping a careful distance struck a chord deep inside me. The uneasy ache that had come into my chest when I'd first seen Cressida and expanded when she'd talked about leaving campus seemed to engulf me completely.

"We don't all need to keep our distance," I said abruptly. "I've been on campus for days, and Cressida hasn't been compelled toward me at all. While she's doing this, at least for her initial investigations, I'm going to ask for a leave of absence from my classes and go with her."

Declan jerked around in his chair. "What are you talking about?"

I waved toward Cressida's image on the laptop screen, my

heart beating faster again, but this time with anticipation rather than horror. "She shouldn't be going out tracking down evidence from the reapers on her own. I can add clout from my position in the pentacle if she needs that backup. The rest of you would be more at risk if you took on that job, and you've also got more on your plates. It only makes sense."

"I'm sure we can make other arrangements," Declan said. "But let's talk about this amongst ourselves—"

My spine stiffened. No, I wasn't letting him hide this conversation from the woman it affected the most. If he was going to deny my right to stand by my girlfriend, then he'd better be prepared to do it to her face.

"Cressida deserves to hear this," I cut in. "And I think I deserve the opportunity to make this choice. I've been as careful as you all asked, and there's been no sign that the spell's targeting me. Cressida and I have already proven we can work well together."

"Is this really about working together?" Malcolm asked with a slightly wry note in his voice. "We know you've got a personal stake there."

"Sure," I said. "She's my girlfriend, and I want to be with her for that reason too. What does that matter? I haven't let our relationship interfere with anything else we've tried to work on. I'm not going to get distracted while we're in the middle of investigating a reaper family or something. If anything, it makes me even more invested in getting this problem solved as quickly as we can."

"We could send a couple of blacksuits with her," Rory started, in a tone less vehement than Declan's had been.

Cressida cleared her throat. "Actually, I don't think

that would work. The staff here already suggested it, but I'm going to need to work some of my old connections, talk to people who are going to be hesitant to open up even to me. If I've got a blacksuit with me, there's no way they'll let anything slip. And the blacksuits have to follow official procedures and all that if it becomes a formal investigation. I'm hoping that keeping things more casual will give me an edge we haven't had before."

"There you go," I said, motioning to my colleagues. "I'd be there as a supporter—as her boyfriend—whatever works. Just don't give me an official order to do any investigating, and we'll have that flexibility."

"Noah," my brother said, his refusal coming through in just those two syllables, and a sudden surge of anger that I hadn't known I had in me flared to the surface.

"Look," I said, "I know this might make me sound unprofessional, but I'm not a full baron yet anyway. *You* of all people should know something about bending the rules and taking risks for someone you love. How 'safe' was it for you to support Rory when all of the old barons were trying to get her under their control? How many times did you put your position as baron-to-be and whatever else on the line so that you could be with her and stand by her?"

Declan winced, a flicker of recognition passing through his eyes. Jude looked like he'd muffled a chuckle. Rory rubbed her hand over her face, but she didn't argue with my assessment.

I knew how much he'd done for her, how far he'd gone, in a position that in many ways had been way more precarious than the one we were in right now. He didn't have a foot to stand on if he tried to tell me that *I* was making the wrong decisions.

"Noah," he said quietly, "I'm only trying to look out for you."

A lump rose in my throat. I tipped my head forward in recognition. "I know. And I understand. But I'm not just your little brother. I'm an adult, I have my own priorities, and I should have the right to make my own decisions. You got the chance to take the risks that seemed worth it to you years ago. I should have that chance too."

And what did it really matter if something happened to me, other than that Declan would feel guilty? I didn't say the words, but they burned a hole in my gut. We didn't *need* another Ashgrave baron. My brother filled that role more than enough.

I was always going to be the second-best, the backup… unless I really struck out on my own and figured out who I could be without his guidance. Maybe then I'd be getting somewhere.

I had no idea how much of what I was thinking Declan might have guessed at. He glanced around the table as if hoping someone might back him up in a way he hadn't come up with, but the other barons and Agnes just gazed back at him. Rory offered a small, sympathetic smile, as if to say, *I know you hate it, but he's got a point.*

Declan exhaled in a rush and turned back to me. I wanted to glance at the laptop and see how Cressida was taking all this, but I didn't dare look away from my brother right now.

He held my gaze for a long moment as if searching my

soul for reassurance. Then he dipped his head. "All right. If you feel that strongly about it, then I'm definitely not in the position to stand in your way." His gaze darted toward Rory again, and something in his expression softened. "I hope taking those chances works out as well for you as it did for me."

11

*Cressida*

Looking around my dorm bedroom with my suitcase open on the bed beside me, I felt as if I'd stepped through some kind of time warp that had yanked me back to the morning before I'd first seen Emeric—when this whole mess with the reapers had been set in motion. Except this time I was in Rory's position, packing up my stuff to go, and Victory was in the role I'd had then, perched on the end of my bed surveying my progress.

"You really don't have much to work with here, do you?" she remarked in an offhand tone—not judgy, just observing.

I sighed. "Splitting off from my parents was kind of a spur-of-the-moment thing, right? I didn't have time to grab any of my stuff from home. And really... it's seemed kind of silly to worry about buying much in the way of clothes or whatever when we have bigger problems."

I folded one last blouse and tucked it into the suitcase. I might not have had a huge wardrobe here at school, but the clothes I'd had on hand were still more and fancier than an awful lot of the other students could afford. I couldn't complain. I just hoped I'd picked out the ones that would be best for the task ahead of me.

Victory hummed to herself. "You've got to look after yourself in little ways as well as the big ones. But I won't badger you about it. As long as you're bringing at least one outfit meant to impress those two suitors you've picked up."

My laugh came out a little choked. "I wish I could pack something that would convince them *not* to come along for the ride."

Victory raised her eyebrows. "Oh, come on. You don't love that they're noble enough to join you on your quest without fear of the danger?"

I grimaced at her. There had been something intoxicating about watching Noah declare his intention of joining me to the other barons. And I guessed if I'd thought about it, I wouldn't really have expected Emeric to stay behind. He'd already graduated; the only thing he cared about on campus was his sister, and helping me would help her too—as he'd pointed out yesterday when we'd talked about my leaving.

But still…

"*I'm* afraid of the danger," I said. "I'm terrified enough for myself without worrying about getting them killed on top of it." I gave Victory a narrow look. "They're not just boy toys or something, you know. I care about them a lot."

I wasn't going to drop the L word around her, but she'd be able to tell I was serious.

"And I'd bet they'd both rather you stayed relatively safe and sound here on campus," Victory pointed out. "But you're making your choice, and they're making theirs. I give them points for making the right one." She grinned at me.

"Right," I muttered. I zipped the suitcase shut and stared down at it, barely seeing it in that moment. Noah and Emeric were going to meet me out at the parking garage in about an hour. The health center staff had insisted on my first face-to-face meeting with the Ashgrave scion happening away from the main activity on campus just in case. They were hanging out in the dorm common room right now, monitoring for any sign of reaper magic reaching out to the spell inside me.

I was definitely not going to miss having several stalkers following my every move.

What if something did go wrong when I got close to Noah? What if the reapers descended on us the second we left campus and tore us all to shreds? I swallowed thickly and reached to touch the conducting piece dangling from a metal chain around my neck like a large pendant.

It should keep me out of the reapers' notice at least a little. Until I started poking my nose into places they didn't want me to go, anyway. But I guessed as long as we could survive whatever they threw at us, we'd learn a lot by seeing what places and people they were the most anxious to defend.

It was that surviving part I wasn't so sure I could pull off.

But that was fine. I drew my spine straighter and managed to smile back at Victory. I was Cressida Warbury, damn it, and I'd survived a hell of a lot already. I was the kind of woman who walked on people, not who got walked on. Even if I was more careful about who I crushed under my feet these days.

"Okay," I said, taking one last look around. "I think that's everything. I'm supposed to wait in the health center until we're all ready to go." The packing hadn't taken as long as I'd allotted for it. I kind of wished I had an excuse to linger here instead of going back to that dull white room, but the staff monitoring me would notice if I seemed to just be sitting around chatting.

"I'll join you," Victory announced, which was generous of her and beyond what I'd ever have asked. At least the room would be less boring with her there to shoot the breeze with while we passed the last stretch of time.

I found the bravado to make a joke out of it. "Not worried I'll blow you up?"

She snorted. "They haven't managed to detonate you so far. I'll take my chances."

As I came out into the common room, the school staff immediately converged around me. "All's well so far," said the doctor who seemed to be in charge of my case. "But let's get you someplace secure for the time being."

I nodded and let them escort me down the stairs to the green, the five of them staying in a loose circle around me and Victory. None of them had complained about *her* presence near me, at least not in my hearing, but I wasn't sure if that was because they weren't as concerned about her as they were about a scion or because she'd already put them in their place.

Knowing Victory, I wouldn't be at all surprised to find out it was the latter.

As I came out of Ashgrave Hall with my entourage, my gaze caught on Hadley just coming along the path from the lake. When our gazes locked, she hesitated, her steps slowing, and then jerked her eyes away. A flicker of fear passed into my chest, and my skin prickled with apprehension.

"Give me a second?" I said to my keepers. "I need to talk to someone. You don't have to be *too* close to do your monitoring, right?"

The doctor's mouth flattened, but she made a gesture of acceptance. As we came off the green onto the wider path, I strode ahead of the group to intercept Hadley.

She'd made a minor attempt at diverting to avoid me, but when she saw me heading right for her, she stopped and squared her shoulders. I pulled my own posture straighter, lifting my chin like I had when I'd been psyching myself up before. If something was going on with her, Cressida the bitch was the one who'd get her to spill the beans.

"Hadley," I said in a cool tone. "What's going on?"

She laughed awkwardly. "I was just coming up from the lake. Taking a break from my first batch of homework. Nothing exciting."

"No? I got the distinct impression that you weren't happy to see me, even though I was just passing by. Which makes me think you didn't want me to come talk to you. Funny how that meant I definitely had to."

Hadley swiped her hand across her mouth. "I don't know what made you think that. It's not like we're friends. Sorry if you think I should have waved or something."

I folded my arms over my chest, thinking of Victory behind me and how she'd handle this situation. "It's not about being friendly. It's about you having secrets you haven't spilled. Did you hear something new from your parents? Or remember something you'd forgotten before? Let's just get it over with. That'll be easier for both of us, don't you think?"

My domineering approach seemed to work just as well as it had two days ago. Hadley sucked in a breath and then shuddered. But whatever she was afraid of in that moment, it wasn't me. "My parents really don't have any idea what the other families are doing, okay? They're just doing business, making a living. They don't have anything against the new barons. Neither do I."

I didn't know how much I believed that, but I'd accept it if she got on to the point. "That's fine. I'm not accusing you or them of anything. Now—what happened?"

Hadley looked at her feet. Her voice dropped too. "It's just more of the same, really. I talked to my parents yesterday after the attack—they were worried, of course— and they mentioned… they mentioned they'd gotten another order of a few animals all at once. Specifically asking for animals with a defiant disposition this time."

Ah. That didn't surprise me, now that she'd mentioned it. The reapers were back to their experiments because they hadn't accounted for how well I'd be able to resist their efforts. I'd be almost proud if the news didn't mean they might be figuring out new strategies to overcome my resistance right now.

"I see," I said. "I think you'd better mention that to the barons too."

Hadley paled even more than she had when I'd first approached her. "What? I—I don't mind if you bring it up—"

I shook my head. "You'll score a lot more points if they hear it directly from you. If I tell them, they'll wonder why *you* didn't. You wouldn't want that, would you?"

"No. No, you're right."

"At the very least, talk to the headmistress about it," I advised, since who knew when the barons would be on campus next. "Was there anything else?"

"Well, I—" She grimaced and met my eyes again. "It was your parents. The ones who placed the order. They did it through one of their employees, but my dad recognized the name."

My pulse stuttered. That revelation I hadn't been quite as prepared for. Mom and Dad were really in the thick of it still. Going out of their way to screw over their only daughter even more.

I schooled my expression to be as impassive as I could manage, tamping down the turmoil rising inside me. All at once, the posturing I'd been doing exhausted me. Being mean was fucking tiring.

And it wasn't even who I was anymore.

"That's good to know," I said, and then, because it couldn't hurt, "Thank you."

I strode back over to Victory and the group of waiting staff, turning the new, unpleasant information over in my head.

Somehow I couldn't shake the feeling that before this was over, I'd be staring down my parents again. I just hoped that this time it wouldn't be with my hands bound and my magic stifled.

*Emeric*

"You can call me any time you want," I said, watching Shauna's face for any sign that she was upset. "I'll have my phone on me at all times. And the reapers shouldn't be able to target the school again the same way." Not if Cressida didn't return until we'd found a fix for the spell on her.

My sister just rolled her eyes. Typical teenager. But weirdly, it made me feel a little better that she was comfortable enough with me now that she'd make that show of dismissiveness rather than trying to stay on her best behavior. She trusted me not to get mad.

"I'll be fine," she said. "I've been fine for more than a year already when you were all the way off in Portland."

I grimaced at her. "The reapers didn't have a bone to pick with me back then. You still need to be more careful than before."

"I'm not the one who pissed them off," she pointed out, folding her arms over her chest and leaning back on the sofa in my temporary campus apartment. Then her tone softened a little. "I know you're worried they'll try to attack me to punish you, but like you said, they shouldn't be able to attack anyone around here with no way to easily get past the wards. I already promised I wouldn't leave campus. I didn't much before anyway. It's not like there's anything so exciting in town."

And we didn't have a home to go back to in Portland anymore, not really. I'd have to get the house cleaned up and sell it for however much I could, and then find a new home somewhere else. Somewhere Shauna could safely visit, at least, even if she wanted to strike out on her own as soon as she was done with school.

How long would it take for either of us to be safe *anywhere* beyond the school wards?

I didn't like thinking about that or the danger I'd be in the second I stepped outside them. I'd known the risks I was taking on when I'd helped Cressida and Noah escape the reapers. It'd been more than worth it. Maybe I'd have to look into getting a teaching gig so this apartment could be more permanent.

Or maybe the new barons would eventually crush the last of the so-called loyalists, and there'd be no one left who wanted my head on a stick to begin with.

I'd get by either way. I just wished my sister hadn't become a target at the same time.

"We'll get through this, like we kept it together after

Dad died," I said. "It can't be forever." I refused to let it be forever.

"Of course it won't be. And I've got six more years of school to get through, so you have plenty of time to figure out how to fix things before it matters all that much to me." She grinned at me a little cheekily to show she was partly joking.

She was right, though, that this was my problem to fix. I'd drawn Cressida into the reapers' orbit. I hadn't figured out what an idiot I was being until it was too late to get her out of their clutches before any damage was done. I hadn't even managed to put the pieces together to realize what they'd done to her until it was almost too late.

At least I'd been there when the spell had hit her—I'd been able to recognize the problem in the moment. If she'd been on her own... she really might have walked right over to the barons' meeting room and blown most of this building sky high.

I shoved down that uncomfortable thought and focused on Shauna again. "I can come by to visit now and then, depending on how far away we have to go to follow the leads that Cressida's found. If there's anything you'd want me to bring back—food you can't get so easily, or new clothes you need or—"

"Do we have enough money for that?" Shauna asked without judgment, just practicality.

I gave her my best older brother look, the one that said that problem was also for me to worry about, not her. "We have enough that I can make sure you have everything you need and a few extras on top of that. I'm not bringing you back a Mercedes, but if there's anything essential or something small that would make you happy, just tell me."

She cocked her head in thought, and a shadow crossed her face. I tensed, waiting for her to speak, but whatever I'd anticipated, it wasn't what she said when she met my eyes again.

"I just want *you* to come back," she murmured. "You'll be careful, right? It's you they're really angry at, and seeing what they did to Cressida—what they tried to do to the school—" She shuddered.

My gut twisted. For the first time since I'd decided I was joining Cressida on her mission to find answers, a jab of real doubt passed through me. I could accept the risks to myself, but I hated the idea of Shauna stressing out over my decision.

She hadn't said it, but we both knew I was the only family she had left.

"Of course I'll be careful," I said. "And the staff said that the protective piece Cressida's going to be wearing should shield all of us within a small radius, so as long as I stay close to her, the reaper families might not even realize I'm out there."

The corners of Shauna's mouth twitched upward. "And I guess it won't be too much trouble for you to stay close to her, huh?"

I glowered at my sister half-heartedly. "Just wait until you get a boyfriend and I can start teasing you about him."

Her smile grew. "What if I get a girlfriend?"

I threw my hands in the air. "Whatever. Equal

opportunity teasing. You're not getting out of it no matter who you end up dating."

She laughed. "I guess that's good to know." She stood up, shaking out her legs after the long time in the same position. "I've got to get to class now. Thank you for talking about all this with me, but I really will be okay while you're gone. You just make sure you stay okay too."

"Right," I said, my throat tightening all over again, and got up to give her a quick hug. Shauna flashed me another smile and headed out.

I watched the door click shut with a weird mix of emotions. I couldn't help still being worried about her, but it felt like I'd gotten something right in our relationship. Which was a particular relief when I'd come so close to screwing that part of my life up too.

Before heading to the parking garage, I walked over to the apartment's bedroom to confirm I'd packed everything I needed. I'd just stepped into the room when something hit the window outside with a wet-sounding *thunk*.

My gaze darted to the glass. A dark blotch that looked like a damp rag had smacked into it and appeared to have stuck there. Then, as I watched, the solid black material seemed to melt into a viscous red liquid. It streaked down the glass like a waterfall of blood.

My pulse stuttered. I froze, torn between marching over to get a better sense of what I was up against and turning tail to run straight to the nearest blacksuits.

The wash of crimson liquid parted. Here and there, it faded to show the plain glass again, in the shape of a series of letters. *TRAITORS PAY.*

An icy finger traced down my spine. It wasn't any mystery who'd have sent that message. I didn't even have to wonder all that hard how it'd been delivered. I'd watched Cressida be assaulted by a "message" her parents had sent the day I'd come to campus to set my plan in motion. Powerful mages could always find a way to sneak small hostile spells past the school's defenses. Nothing that would actually hurt anyone, but the thing on my window was likely just an illusion.

It was already fading completely away, leaving no evidence that it'd been there at all. I stared at the window for several beats longer in case anything else would reveal itself.

There might be traces of the spell lingering on the glass. I'd have to stop by the headmistress's office on my way out and let Ms. Grimsworth know that the blacksuits should investigate it.

Not that I really thought whoever had sent that message would have been careless enough to leave any hint that would reveal their identity.

If I'd been at all unsure about the reapers' current feelings about me, that demonstration made things pretty clear. I drew in a breath, steadying my nerves, and went to grab my suitcase like I'd intended to in the first place.

I couldn't let our enemies intimidate me into backing down. I'd spent too much of my life catering to their wants and opinions and never giving myself a chance to form my own. If the reapers wanted to take me on, let them try. I'd at least make them pay a little on my way down.

Pulling my wheeled suitcase, I went down the hall and gave Ms. Grimsworth a brief report on the spell I'd just witnessed. Her mouth pulled tight as I spoke, but she sent me off with just a confirmation that she'd have the security staff investigate. We'd already discussed my decision to leave campus yesterday, and she wasn't going to try to stop me now.

Downstairs, I was just passing through the grand hall when a tall, broad-shouldered figure with distinctive authoritative bearing caught my eye. Malcolm Nightwood —Baron Nightwood, as I really should think of him now even in the privacy of my head—was striding across the polished floor from the opposite direction, almost straight toward me.

My first instinct was to get as far out of his way as I possibly could. The Nightwoods had a definite reputation both at Blood U and in the wider fearmancer community, and while the current baron had turned against his even more brutal parents, I'd heard about plenty of brutality on his part even when he was just a junior while I was still attending classes here. He wasn't someone I had any interest in crossing.

Before I could make good on that intention, though, Malcolm's gaze caught on me. He veered toward me, slowing as he moved to intercept me.

I stopped, a knot of apprehension forming in my stomach. Had he come specifically to see me—did he have a problem with me leaving campus? Maybe some of the barons felt I couldn't be trusted, considering I'd only just switched loyalties to their side a little while ago.

But the baron gave me a slight yet genuine-looking smile and tipped his head toward my suitcase. "Riplowe. You're about to set off with Cressida, huh?" His low voice managed to sound commanding even when he was making a casual observation.

I nodded. "We didn't want to delay very long, considering the situation. I—I didn't realize you'd be on campus, baron." I caught myself just shy of saying I hadn't thought it was safe. It didn't seem wise to question a baron's ability to make his own risk assessment.

Malcolm could probably pick up on that undercurrent to my statement anyway. He just chuckled. "You can call me Malcolm. 'Baron' is for if you need to plead for forgiveness. And I believe you'd already done that with Cressida, who's the one you really owed it to anyway."

I'd apologized in front of the full pentacle of barons too, but maybe he had so many meetings and so many people to intimidate he didn't remember that. "By some miracle, she forgave my sins," I said.

That remark made Malcolm laugh again. Then his gaze turned more intent. My hackles started to rise, anticipating some kind of jab.

He took me by surprise again. "I know what it's like going up against people you used to look up to and want to impress," he said, still firm but with an unmistakable note of earnestness. "It feels like shit a lot of the time, and you're always wondering if you're making yourself just as bad as they are. I don't know how to avoid all that, but I can tell you that it's a lot better on the other side. It's better to fight and know you gave it your best shot than to let them call the shots."

For a second, I didn't know what to say. I never would have related my experience to that of the barons—but I guessed it wasn't all that different. Only Malcolm's situation had been worse. He'd had to take on his own parents, like Cressida.

But he'd thought it was worth sharing that experience with me, like I was an equal. Like he wanted me to succeed.

I couldn't quite wrap my head around that generosity, but the tension that'd gripped me the second I saw him released. I smiled back without having to force it. "I'm sure it is. I don't have any intention of rolling over."

"Good man," Malcolm said, giving my shoulder a light cuff. "Take care of Cressida, and make sure Noah doesn't get any ideas that're too big."

He walked off, and I stood there for a second absorbing the moment before I set off for the garage, this time with my heart a little lighter.

13

*Cressida*

The second I saw Noah standing by my Mustang, my heart leapt to my throat. Through no conscious intent at all, my body propelled me into his arms.

"Hey," he said in a voice that sounded a little choked, hugging me close. I clung to him as tightly as I could without feeling totally pathetic and then forced myself to ease back. He didn't waste a second leaning in to capture my mouth with a deep, sweet kiss.

It'd been less than a week since I'd last seen him, but after spending so much time together in the month before that and sharing so much, his absence had felt like a torturous year.

When Noah pulled back, he kept one hand on my waist and glanced past me to Emeric, who'd come up behind me. "Good to see you too," he said with a grin. "I hope you'll forgive me if I don't offer quite as enthusiastic a greeting as I did to our girlfriend."

A startled laugh broke out of Emeric, leaving him smiling back. Any tension that might have hovered in the air between my two boyfriends vanished just like that.

"I have no problem at all with that," he said, and nodded to my car. "Should we get going?"

"Are you riding with Cressida?" Noah asked. His Mazda was parked in the spot next to mine.

Emeric nodded. "I wanted to leave my car for my sister in case she needs it. And it seems like it'll be safest for all of us if I stay within range of Cressida's conducting piece as much as possible. I don't know how determined the reapers are about getting revenge on me, but… they've made it clear they haven't forgotten how I turned on them."

"You'd think they'd take a hint from how many people have turned away from them that maybe they're doing something a little bit wrong," I muttered, and sighed. "It's fine. I'm glad to have the company—from both of you." I tipped forward to steal another quick kiss from Noah. "But we'd better head out before the staff get too worried that I'll blow up the whole parking garage or something."

Noah's jaw tightened at my remark, but he dipped his head in acknowledgement. "I looked into Sinclair's typical schedule like you asked. She's working for the firm her parents own in Boston. It'll take a couple of days to drive out there, and then we can catch her by the company building. Maybe after work, so we don't have to worry about anyone noticing she's late."

"Sounds good." I exhaled in a rush. "Then there's just the matter of where we'll stop for the night—"

Noah's grin came back. "Oh, I already took care of that."

Something about his smile made me instantly suspicious, but in a good way. "What are you up to?"

He bumped his elbow against mine teasingly. "You'll see when we get there. Just follow my car."

I climbed into the driver's seat of the Mustang and settled in behind the wheel. Emeric took in the smooth leather seats and sleek interior styling and let out a low whistle. "I'm not sure I've gotten to ride in a car this nice before."

I rolled my eyes. "My parents' cars are twice as posh. I've had this one for four years... had to keep up appearances back then. But it does also handle *very* well."

It would have been faster to get to Boston by plane. A few years ago, I could have borrowed the Warburys' private jet to make the trip. But being locked in a frame of steel hundreds of miles above the ground hadn't seemed like the most secure option, and I'd rather have my own car on hand for whatever side trips we needed to make. I wasn't deluding myself into thinking we'd get all the answers we needed from my former friend. We'd be lucky if we got any answers at all.

Noah pulled out of the parking garage ahead of us. His raccoon familiar poked its furry face over the top of the back seat and waggled a paw as if waving at us. I focused on Percy soaring along overhead for a moment.

*It's going to be a long trip*, I thought at him, knowing

the gist of my message would get across even if my familiar couldn't understand my exact words. *Pace yourself as much as you need to.*

My familiar replied with a waft of determined reassurance. He didn't plan on letting me out of his sight any more than my human companions did.

Keeping the back of Noah's car in view, I followed him through the town just outside campus and along the various rural roads until we reached the nearest highway heading east. The roar of the engine as we picked up speed made my pulse hiccup, but nothing bad had happened so far. No ambushes had been waiting just outside Blood U. I hadn't exploded yet.

We were only just getting started, but it seemed like a promising beginning.

We drove for most of the day, pausing only to make pit stops and to grab a quick lunch. I let Emeric switch off the driving partway through to give myself a break. Noah insisted he was holding up just fine. "I once drove all the way from Paris to Rome in one night," he informed me. "This is a piece of cake."

When we diverted from the route heading to Boston, the Ashgrave scion led us on a winding route for about a quarter of an hour until we arrived at a sprawling Georgian style building with a sign out front proclaiming it the Lilac Springs Hotel and Spa. My eyebrows rose and stayed arched until he'd parked outside what appeared to be a small private chalet that was part of the property.

"This is an investigative mission, not a holiday," I reminded him as we got out of our cars.

He aimed a little smirk at me. "I don't see why it can't be both. You've been prodded and shut away here and there for days now. I figured you deserved a chance to relax and get a little pampering."

Emeric offered a soft hum. "I can agree with that sentiment."

Noah gave him a light cuff to the shoulder. "*You* could probably use a vacation too."

I touched the conducting piece resting against my sternum. "I don't know how much use I can make of the spa while keeping this on me."

"Not a problem," Noah announced. "We've got everything we need right in the chalet. I even arranged for them to have dinner waiting for us."

He tapped a key code into the panel by the door, and we stepped into a lush room of hardwood paneling mixed with painted walls and furniture in warm, earthy tones. The sight was instantly soothing, and I appreciated it even more with the scent of subtle wine sauce lacing the room.

Our dinner was spread out on the mahogany table at one end of the space next to a compact kitchenette with marble countertops. The plates were all covered with domes, the bottle of chardonnay still corked. When I lifted the cover on my meal, I found the metal was still hot to the touch. Noah had timed our arrival perfectly with the instructions he'd given.

I kicked my shoes off my tired feet and flopped into one of the dining chairs. We all dug in, and soon were reveling in the food so fervently we didn't say much, mostly just made approving and swooning sounds. When the main course was finished, Noah checked the countertop and brought over a white pastry box, a triumphant smile on his face.

I guessed what the box contained before he even opened it. When he revealed the plump eclairs, my mouth started watering even as affection swelled around my heart. "Of course. But will they live up to your favorite bakery? I mean, I'm not picky, but you have pretty exacting standards."

The Ashgrave scion chuckled. "We'll see, but even if they're not quite on par, I didn't have much choice. This is our thing."

I wasn't quite the pastry connoisseur he was, and to my taste buds, the dessert was excellent. When I'd finished it and was licking the last traces of sugar from my lips, I noticed Noah was still looking sly.

"What?" I demanded. "Is there *more*?"

He got up and motioned for the two of us to follow him. "If I'd just wanted to give you a nice dinner, we could have done that at a restaurant."

He led us from the chalet's main room with its lounge area and kitchenette into a massive bedroom the same size as the one we'd just left. A sprawling four-poster king stood at one end of the room… and at the other, an immense whirlpool bathtub rose from a tiled section of floor. It was already full of water and bubbling gently.

I walked over and dipped my hand under the frothy surface. The water lapped at my fingers, the perfect steamy temperature. "Okay," I said. "You've really outdone yourself. You didn't need to splurge like this."

"I could afford it," Noah said. He approached me from behind and slipped his arms around my waist, pressing a kiss to my shoulder. "It doesn't come close to making up for the fact that I couldn't be around while you've been dealing with this awful mess, but… it's something." He paused, the corners of his mouth quirking upward again. "And I suspect both me and Emeric will enjoy this indulgence a lot too."

I glanced at Emeric, whose eyes had widened with an eager gleam, but he hesitated when he looked back at the two of us. The one time we'd all gotten it on together, it'd been a spur of the moment thing, building gradually without us knowing for sure how far we'd go until we got there. This felt more planned, more of a conscious decision.

But it was their decision. I remembered Victory dismissing my concerns about the two guys joining me at all, and my spine drew a little straighter. They wanted to be here with me; Noah had wanted to offer me this extravagance. If he thought I deserved it, then I did.

And I could show them what I wanted too.

I eased out of Noah's embrace and reached to tug off my blouse. "Might as well get as much use out of it as we can, right?" I said.

Noah made an approving sound and reached to unclasp my bra for me. The chalet's warm air teased over my skin. I left on the conducting piece, since there were no spa staff here to complain about it, and reached to my waist. As I shimmied out of my slacks, the Ashgrave heir stripped off his own clothes.

Emeric hesitated for a few beats longer and then said, like he had before he'd kissed me in front of Noah the first time, "Fuck it." He pulled off the gloves he'd donned after we'd left campus, revealing the gleaming metal of his titanium hand and forearm, and pulled off his shirt.

I sank into the water first, a sigh escaping me as the liquid warmth closed around my naked body. I positioned myself so a jet massaged the back of my neck and let my eyes drift shut for a moment. The water burbled as the guys got in on either side of me.

For several minutes, we just lounged there, absorbing the relaxing warmth and releasing the stress of the day. But a starker heat quickly collected low in my belly. I knew Noah had more in mind than this when he arranged for this luxury. Not that he'd be pushy about his advances— but the fact was, it'd been too long since I'd been with him in every possible way.

I pushed myself through the water toward him, settling onto his lap. He gazed at me with eyes gone dark with desire in the moment before I brought my mouth to his.

We kissed, slick and with growing urgency, as the bubbles tickled over my skin. Noah savored the first few kisses, focusing only on them, before turning his attention to other parts of me as well.

As he stroked one hand down my chest, swiveling his thumb over my nipple with a jolt of pleasure that made it pebble in an instant, the water shifted around us again. Emeric came to a stop next to me, caressing me from my shoulder down my side to my hip.

I turned my head to kiss my other lover just as hard. He added his hands to the mix, his metal fingers offering a contrasting texture that left me giddy. When he dipped that hand between my legs, the flare of heat his touch set off brought an undignified whine to my throat.

"I definitely think our woman needs more pampering," he murmured to Noah.

"Hmm." Noah ran his fingers over my thighs and tugged me closer to him. I barely heard the whisper of the protective spell as his fingertips skimmed over my slit. I arched into him instinctively, the hunger to be filled gripping me, and he thrust inside me at just the right angle to make me moan.

Resting my knees on the same ledge he was perched on at the side of the tub, I rocked up and down over him. Bliss surged through me faster than I'd ever experienced it before. As Noah grasped my hip to help guide my angle and rhythm, Emeric conjured more heady sparks in my chest and all the way down to my clit. I kissed him wildly over my shoulder and then kissed Noah again before my breath fractured into pants.

This was what it was all for—all the pain, all the fears, all the horrible futures that might lie ahead. I might not have much life left, but damn, was I getting a good one while it lasted. Somehow these two men, both incredible in their own ways, saw something incredible in me too, and not only that, they were willing to share it with each other.

Emeric's thumb flicked over my clit again, Noah plunged into me, and I came apart, gasping and shuddering, clenching around the scion's still rigid cock. "That's right," he murmured, not hesitating in his thrusts. "Come as hard as you can, and then come again."

I was going to if he kept this pace up. But I didn't want Emeric to be neglected.

When the wave of ecstasy faded enough for me to follow the urge, I lifted off Noah, tugging him with me at the same time. As I turned in front of him, I nudged Emeric toward the side of the tub. "Sit on the edge."

A glint of understanding came into his eyes. He sank onto the lip around the tub, and I splayed my legs so Noah could penetrate me again from behind.

With his first thrust, my eyes rolled back, the pleasure already building fast. But I kept my head enough to remember my other mission.

I wrapped my fingers around Emeric's jutting erection just above the level of the water, loving the way his head tipped back at my firm strokes. His lips parted with a groan. Then I lowered my head to take him into my mouth.

"Fuck," he muttered at the swirl of my tongue around his cock's head. I'd never actually done this before, but he tasted good, with a faint tang from the water and a hint of salt from his precum. I bobbed my head lower, experimenting until I found a rhythm and motion that made his fingers tighten in my hair even more.

His cock throbbed in my mouth, and Noah plunged into me from behind. The whole world seemed to narrow down into a maelstrom of passion. I became nothing but the rush of bliss washing through me and the joint motions of our bodies.

My second orgasm swept over me with a sudden cresting of pleasure. My mouth tightened around Emeric's cock with a muffled moan, and he came with a stuttered breath. As the salty fluid filled my mouth, Noah let out a groan behind me, his hips jerking as he found his release inside me.

I swallowed, pleased that I'd apparently given a satisfactory performance with my first blow job. Emeric dropped back into the water to kiss me on the lips, long and lingering without any sign that he cared where my mouth had been just moments ago.

We settled into a combined embrace against the wall of the tub, me half on Noah's lap and half on Emeric's, and for the next little while, everything was right in our little piece of the world. I only wished I could hold off all the trouble that must lie ahead of us.

*Cressida*

The building that housed the Shadewicks' political consulting firm in Boston was several stories high with mirrored sides that blazed in the late afternoon sunlight. It looked like exactly the kind of place I could imagine Sinclair aspiring to work in. She probably checked her reflection in the panes every time she walked up to the doors, confirming that she looked better than everyone around her—by her standards, at least.

With it being her parents' company, I guessed she wasn't too worried about following typical protocol or showing what a hard worker she was. We'd been able to gather that she often left for the day early, so thankfully I was already staked out down the street when she breezed past the doors at a quarter to four in the afternoon.

She sauntered along the sidewalk, probably off to do

some shopping before heading home, and I hurried after her through the scattered pedestrians passing by on the downtown street. From behind, she could have been the same girl I'd once spent most of my waking hours with back at Blood U. Her smooth black hair was shaped into a typical bob only slightly longer than it'd been before, and she wore a trim dove-gray pantsuit with a couple of splashes of scarlet in her belt and bracelet. She'd always liked the dramatics of pairing a black-and-white color scheme with red.

It had only been two years, after all. I could assume not a whole lot had changed with her. She definitely hadn't made the same attitude re-evaluation that Victory and I had gone through. Now it was just a matter of whether her old ways and my new ones would make it harder or easier for me to get what I wanted.

I caught up with Sinclair just as she reached the corner, tapping her elbow to get her attention. My nerves stayed on high alert as her head snapped toward me, first with a flash of annoyance in her eyes and then with a flicker of shock. She *was* on the reapers' side, no matter how long we'd been friends before that, and I didn't trust her any more than I did my parents. For the same reason, Noah and Emeric were staying close by, hidden by an illusion to deflect her notice, ready to spring in with defensive spells if need be.

Not that they'd necessarily get in there fast enough if she did go on the attack. I had to be ready to protect myself.

For now, Sinclair simply stalled in her tracks and

turned to stare at me. "Cressida? What the—What are you doing here?"

With the last question, she smoothed the confusion out of her voice and managed to sound disdainful, as if I should be ashamed of myself for showing my face anywhere near her. I forced a tight smile, knowing *I* didn't look all that different from how I had the last time we'd hung out together either. It was my loyalties she had an issue with, not my appearance.

"Can't a girl want to catch up with an old friend?" I said, keeping my voice firmly neutral. "I was hoping we could grab a coffee and have a little chat."

Sinclair's eyes narrowed. She took a step back as if she was worried I was going to attack her, but only a faint whiff of anxiety passed from her into me. She wasn't anywhere near as easily cowed as Hadley had been, but then, I hadn't expected her to be.

"There's nothing I'd want to talk about with you," she announced.

I'd been prepared for her to refuse. When we'd been Victory's inner circle, it'd been Victory who'd called the shots, and the two of us had really just been along for the ride. I'd never had any authority over Sinclair, social or otherwise.

But she sure had bowed to Victory's whims, even more than I ever had. The former queen bee's advice might serve me even better here than it had with Hadley in the long run.

I cocked my head in my best impression of Victory's haughty bemusement when someone defied her—just before she laid down the law—and let a bit of steel creep into my tone. "But *I* have a lot of things I'd like to talk about with you. And considering my parents could crush yours and you in an instant, I think you should want to have that conversation."

Sinclair sputtered a laugh. "Like your parents would do anything for you. They *hate* you." Her gaze darted from my eyes to my mouth for just an instant, but that was all the confirmation I needed that she was perfectly aware of the spell they'd planted on me. The spell she'd almost certainly helped create.

I shrugged as if I wouldn't care even if my parents were standing over me right now with an enchanted knife. "Sure. But imagine if they find out that you had the chance to get information on my activities for them and you passed up the opportunity because you were too scared. You *aren't* scared of me, are you, Sinclair? What do you really think I could do to you?"

I didn't have any intention of hurting her, but I let the question drip with promise, an implicit threat that maybe I'd change my mind if she didn't cooperate and that there were all kinds of ways I could make her regret that decision. A slightly sharper flicker of fear coursed into me, but I suspected it was the point about my parents and getting information that won her over. Her jaw tensed, and then she nodded.

"All right," she said. "But I'm picking the place. There's a mage-run café a few blocks from here where we can be sure no one will disturb us."

My instinctive wariness kicked back in at full force. A

mage-run establishment also meant that Sinclair would need to be less careful what magic she used, and Noah and Emeric wouldn't be able to conceal themselves as easily. But I didn't have a better spot in mind. Maybe Sinclair's lips would be a little looser if she thought she'd scored a point.

The things I wanted to know, she wasn't likely to spill anyway. I was going to have to read around the answers she actually gave me, like that glance at my enchanted tooth.

Sinclair led the way down the street and around a corner to a dark-walled café full of varnished wood furniture. It was more old-fashioned than her typical tastes, but who knew whether she actually came here often or had only picked it because she knew of the owners. I watched her carefully the whole way there and as we sat down at a table, making sure she wasn't carrying out any surreptitious castings.

I suspected that my best chance of getting answers was to put her off-balance. Our butts had barely touched the seats when I leaned my elbows onto the table and said, "So they roped you into playing with animals, huh?"

My jab hit the mark. Sinclair's face twitched with a mix of embarrassment and surprise. She schooled her expression into a bland mask a second later, but I knew what I'd seen. She had been actively working on this new casting approach with the other reaper families.

"I don't see how that's any of your business," she said stiffly, and turned to the waitress who'd come over. She ordered a latte.

I asked for a cappuccino and immediately went back on the offensive. "How the hell is it not my business when you helped set me up with a deadly spell inside me?"

Sinclair huffed. "It's not as if I had anything to do with that. I'm on the right side, the side of the loyalists, and when they ask for a few favors, of course I'm going to give them. They know what they're doing. I know better than to stick my nose in too far."

"Sounds like an easy way to get used," I said. "I wonder how many other awful things you've had a hand in without even realizing it."

She glared at me. "Awful depends on who you're talking to, doesn't it? After the way you turned on the real barons, did you really expect to go unpunished?"

"The current barons are the real barons by every standard of fearmancer law," I had to point out. "They won the right to rule fair and square, and unless you're an idiot, you're perfectly aware that their parents attacked *them* first. But if you figure self-defense is a crime, then I guess it's okay with you if I blow you up right now without you even trying to stop me, huh?"

From the jolt of fear that hit me and the twitch of her eyelids, she thought I might really be able to do that. Interesting. Did she just not have any idea how the full spell worked—or did she know that I should be able to control it if I figured out the right way to?

Her body language didn't give away that she expected me to make any specific move with that threat. After a second, she tossed her hair back. "We'll just have to agree to disagree. If you only wanted to argue about the barons, I don't see much point in continuing the conversation."

I shook my head. "No, I'm more interested in who else was wrangling those animals with you. Where you were wrangling them. Surely your family didn't welcome reapers onto your own property while they had plans to upend the current barons in the works? The blacksuits would have a field day with that."

"It wasn't some conspiracy," Sinclair retorted with obvious annoyance. "There's nothing illegal about experimenting with magical techniques. Even if we had worked on it on one of our own properties, it's not like we designed anything specifically to target barons. You're a perfect example of that."

So it hadn't been on Shadewick ground. "They were still working toward their big plan. You can't dodge responsibility that easily."

Sinclair snorted. "You do think highly of yourself, don't you? You're not part of any big plan. Your parents saw the opportunity to work with what they'd made and jumped on it. As far as I know, they hadn't even been thinking—"

She snapped her mouth shut, cutting herself off as if she'd realized she'd said more than she'd meant to. I had to restrain a smile even though my stomach listed queasily in the same moment.

Could it be true that the reapers hadn't had a specific scheme to take on the barons yet when I'd fallen into their hands? I'd just become a convenient instrument to build a scheme around. And from what Sinclair was suggesting, it'd been my parents calling a lot of the shots.

Maybe they weren't just one of many families working together. Maybe they were the masterminds behind this whole effort.

A chill ran down my back. "So nice to know you've been supporting my parents while their real daughter was AWOL," I said, putting on an edge of sarcasm in the hopes of provoking her more.

Sinclair raised her chin. "I know how to make alliances, unlike *some* people."

"And my parents are really the best family you could ally yourself with?"

"If I want to have a good place in the new rule, I think so."

I might have wondered why she was admitting her goals and how my parents figured in so bluntly, except at the same moment I caught the faint movement of her lips and a subtle gesture under the table. She was trying to add me to the list of favors she'd offered my parents.

In the corner where we were sitting, I didn't have much room to maneuver. I dove off the chair with as much force as I could, the spell she'd been casting snagging on my sleeve just shy of wrapping around my wrist. She'd probably meant to lock all my limbs in place.

I spun around, crouched on the floor, focusing my mental shields against any attempt she might make to penetrate them with a persuasive spell. Simultaneously, I spat out a casting word of my own, one I'd kept in the back of my throat in case our conversation ended like this.

The illusion didn't change anything in the real world. All it did was convince Sinclair that she couldn't see, hear, or feel anything around her, blanking out all her senses.

She went rigid in her chair, swaying a little as she fought for balance now that she didn't have any physical sensations to guide her. "Cressida," she snarled.

I'd always been way better with illusions than she was, but that didn't mean I'd be able to hold her like this for long. I straightened up, backing away so I was farther out of range if she tried to cast at me. A presence came up beside me—Noah, I could tell without looking at him.

"Thank you for that chat," I said to Sinclair. "Sorry you'll have to disappoint my parents."

I fished a couple of bills out of my purse and handed them to the waitress who was just bringing over our coffee and had stopped to stare with widened eyes. Then I stalked out of the café without another word.

*Cressida*

"Just how many properties does your family own?" Emeric asked, peering through the windshield as I drove down the quiet country lane. Noah was following in his car right behind us.

I swiped my hand across my mouth, not entirely comfortable with the question. "Just remember that *I* don't have any stake in any of these places now that my parents have disowned me. I think it's about ten. At least five around the New England area and then a few scattered vacation properties internationally."

When he raised his eyebrows, I shot him a pointed look. "It's not actually that extravagant by the standards of the top fearmancers. I'm sure all of the barons own at least twice that much. The Warburys are just on par with people of our—their—'standing.'"

"Well, I'd rather be in your company even if you don't

own any fancy estates," Emeric said with a lightly teasing tone that brought down my hackles. "Why are we checking out this one?"

I exhaled in a rush. "It's the most isolated out of all the private Warbury holdings in this region. We didn't come out here all that often, so hopefully we won't run into my parents while we're there." Noah had talked to his brother before we'd set off, and Declan had been able to confirm via the blacksuits that my parents had been spotted recently going about their business two states away. "And because it's isolated, it's the place they were most likely to experiment with magic."

This time Emeric's eyes widened with surprise that was legit rather than playful. "Did they go around inventing horrifying new techniques a lot?"

I let out a rough chuckle. "No, mostly they weren't outright inventing anything, just testing the limits of certain spells or perfecting the approach they wanted to take when they were planning a major casting that'd be in front of other fearmancers. But if they did any personal work related to the casting that's on me, which it's sounding like they did, they'd probably have come out here."

"And we'll be able to look around without setting off any magical booby traps or similar?"

"We'll have to be careful," I admitted. "But I know their approach to security, and I don't think they'll have considered that I might come back to any of their properties. They think I'm running scared. Sinclair isn't likely to report back to them that I'm poking around asking questions when then she'll have to admit that she gave away more than she should have."

He flexed his titanium hand, back in its glove while we were out in the wider world. "Well, if we need to handle anything potentially lethal, I've got the perfect tool right here."

His momentary good humor faded quickly. I couldn't help thinking of the last time he'd needed to use that hand to destroy a spell—and the animal that spell was attached to.

"Does it still hurt?" I asked tentatively. "The broken familiar bond?"

Emeric shrugged, his gaze veering back to the window. "Just mild twinges now and then at this point. But I miss having him—having that connection. There really is something special about it, isn't there?"

I thought of Percy, flying along overhead, a little confused by all the traveling we'd been doing but dedicated to keeping up with me all the same. "Yeah, there is. I guess when you're totally healed, you could find another. Rory ended up taking a new familiar several months after her first one passed."

He nodded, and we sat in silence for several minutes. A hunched oak tree that I recognized came into view up ahead. I slowed a little, put on my signal—even though there was no real traffic—to let Noah know we'd be turning, and swung onto an even smaller private road that led to the gate to the Warbury country home.

A prickle of uneasiness ran over my skin as I parked outside the gate and got out of the car. I'd never seen the stone arch and solid wrought-iron door up close on foot. My parents had always cast the gate open so we could drive right inside. The opaque black surface loomed ominously over us, offering no glimpse of what lay on the other side.

Noah parked behind my car and stepped out. "Do you need any help?"

"Not yet," I said. "Their spells are usually tuned to our bloodline. Lucky for me, I'm still a Warbury by birth even if they don't consider me one of their own anymore."

I spoke a few cautious casting words to feel out the vibe of the magic around the gate and along the wall. Several defensive spells twined together on the gate itself. Most of them would alert my parents if they were disturbed in the wrong way. I definitely didn't want that.

I bit my lip, considering my options. I could tell what sorts of commands would unwind the protections as if the owners were opening things up, but I wasn't sure I had the magical power to pull it off. There was quite a bit of physicality magic woven in.

"Emeric," I said, "do you remember when we got stuck in that little gully in the forest? You lent a little magic to an illusion I made so that you'd get some of the benefit of the fear it provoked."

Emeric nodded with a grimace. Our trials in the woods hadn't been the most enjoyable adventure. "What about it?"

"I'm thinking we should try something similar. There are physical pieces in the gate that need to be adjusted in a particular way—I can see how, but I might not have enough control to pull it off. I'll use my magic to guide yours to the right place and show you what to do, and then you give it the final push." I paused. "The only downside is that if we mess up, the backlash will hit you as well as me."

Emeric rolled his shoulders. "I'm ready to take that gamble. Let's do it."

I glanced back at Noah. "You should keep an eye out for any new magical effects that might become active while we're working on this. I'll be concentrating so hard I might not realize."

"Got it," Noah said with a little salute, but his expression was serious. He knew what my parents were like and just how vindictive their security spells might be if we triggered them.

I focused on the gate again, tracing my awareness over the intricate whorls of the spells as I murmured more casting words. Then I extended a tendril of magic toward Emeric. He added his own voice to the mix, a wave of his energy tingling through my chest.

There were a couple of elements I needed to handle myself. I concentrated on the aspects of the defensive casting that were keyed to the Warbury family line and pushed my essence toward them. They slowly unfurled from the mass of spells. I let out a breath. That was the easiest part.

Here and there in the gate, little mechanisms were set to fire off destructive magical effects if prodded wrong. They all needed to be released for us to get inside. I started at the top left, concentrating until I had a clear sense of the structure and which way to twist it, and then projected that image to Emeric.

He cast his magic forward, winding through mine but now taking the lead. Alongside him, I felt when the mechanism gave, the spell lodged in it relaxing.

It was going to be *so* much fun putting all this back in order when we were leaving. But I couldn't let myself worry about anything that far ahead yet.

I moved to the next section and then the next, repeating the process with Emeric. Other than our casting words, we remained silent, as did Noah. The gate was in full sunlight, and the end-of-summer heat combined with the effort had me sweating soon enough. A droplet ran over my scalp. I didn't want to adjust my focus for even long enough to wipe my forehead.

At the last section, I could sense Emeric's energy starting to flag too. I clenched my hands, willing all of my attention onto the final piece. His contribution shivered through my awareness. There was a slight hitch, and my pulse hiccupped—but then the piece shifted the way it was meant to. The doors swung open without any of us meeting a horrible end.

Emeric laughed raggedly and swiped his sweat-damp hair back from his forehead. "Your parents do know their security systems."

"Good thing they don't know *me* as well as they thought they did," I replied, and strode in through the gate.

I wasn't naïve enough to think that the gate would be the only challenge. My parents liked to place a few alarms in somewhat random places where only they'd know to disarm them. But those were all totally keyed to the family bloodline, so all I had to do was locate them and turn them off. I found one in a rock a short distance down the front drive and another invisible casting that seemed to dangle from a tree branch near the garage.

Noah and Emeric looked around, taking in the property. A low stone cottage stood off to one side, with the garage—which used to be a carriage house—just a few steps away. There were a couple of smaller stone outbuildings farther across the field, but mostly the property was typical country terrain.

"I know it doesn't look like much," I said. "My family never bothered to pretty it up a lot since we don't come out here often. They mostly held on to it so they had a place no one had ever paid much attention to for when they wanted to get up to things that they particularly didn't want noticed."

"Sounds like the perfect spot to be experimenting with dangerous new magic, then," Noah said. "Where do we start?"

"I'm not sure," I admitted. I eyed the cottage, thinking of the conductive piece that might still be displayed inside with the maker's name on the bottom—but I no longer believed that finding my parents' accomplices would help us anywhere near as much as figuring out what my parents themselves might have been doing. And they'd have additional security on the home.

I turned toward the broader field. "I doubt they'd have been working with destructive spells inside the buildings, so let's wander around the grounds and see if we turn anything up there. They'd have covered up any evidence from whatever tests they conducted, but they wouldn't have been as careful while on our own private property as they might have anywhere else. It's possible that they missed something that'd be useful to us."

We skirted the garage and spread out, Noah walking about ten feet to my left and Emeric the same at my right. I'd warned them to keep an eye out for more random alarms, so they murmured periodic casting words as they went. I spoke my own, alongside additional spells designed to pick up various sorts of magic. If my parents had worked on their new spell around here, had they left any traces behind?

We'd just come up on one of the outbuildings, what had probably been a live-in gardener's house at some point, when one of my attempts brought a quiver of a response into my chest. I paused, studying the ground around us a little more intently.

I couldn't pick up on any other hints of magical activity, but there were different types of signs. "Does the grass here look a little greener than the rest?" I asked the guys.

They stopped to consider it. "I think so," Noah said. "You figure they magically encouraged new growth?"

"If they were exploding animals and who knows what else, they'd probably have needed to." I stalked around the perimeter of the area, bending closer here and there to check for any kind of marking or other evidence that might offer more clues.

The grass all looked perfectly normal... other than being almost perfect. I wet my lips and started to straighten up when my gaze snagged on a pale object wedged under the window of the gardener's cottage.

I walked over and tugged it out. It was a torn slip of paper, most of it singed, with just a couple of handwritten words visible on it: *check Bernice*. From the ragged edges around the writing, that was the middle of the sentence. It wasn't much, but my spirits lifted abruptly.

Emeric came up beside me. "Who's Bernice? Maybe she knows something about this spell?"

A slight smile curved my lips. "Bernice isn't really a *who* but a *what*. My parents have a bookcase in the library of old, rare books on magical technique, some of them the only remaining editions. One of them was by this mage named Bernice Something-or-other. I've heard them brag about it before—how they managed to track down the last surviving copy. They must have been using that book to help them figure out the spell."

Noah brightened. "Which means if we read the book, it might help us figure out how they put the elements together too."

"Exactly. Of course, that book is in the main Warbury residence. I can't imagine them risking taking it off the property. And I don't—"

A bolt of magic shuddered across the back of my neck, and I stiffened. My Warbury blood thumped faster with a nearly inaudible siren no one else would have been able to hear. Shit.

"Come on!" I said, yanking at the guys. "An alarm's gone off—we have to get out of here."

We took off for the gate, our feet pelting over the grass as fast as we could go. The wrought-iron door groaned, but because Warbury magic had opened it, the spell that might have slammed it shut was clashing with the intent I'd put into unlocking it. We raced even faster, dashing up the drive and through the gateway just as the door started to swing.

It clanged into place behind us, loud enough that I jumped. We scrambled into our cars. "Head that way," I told Noah, pointing toward the country road we'd arrived on. "The nearest town is over there, about a half hour away. We need to get mixed in with other people. If we're out on the roads and the only ones around, any security people who show up will home right in on us."

I dove into the driver's seat and started the ignition. As Emeric yanked his door shut, I hit the gas. We tore up the gravel road, the tiny rocks rattling against the undercarriage.

The place's isolation worked in our favor. Whatever employees my parents might have called in were too far away to get to the estate immediately. I didn't spot any other vehicles in the rearview mirror during the entire hurried drive into town.

We parked at the curb across from a bank and got out to take stock. Noah laughed a little, his eyes sparkling with the excitement of the escape now that the threat was less imminent. "It's definitely always exciting around you," he said. Kato poked his raccoon face out the open window, chittering as if in agreement.

"Right," I grumbled. "My parents will probably figure out it was me, considering the way I disabled the security systems. But I don't think they can get any more pissed off at me than they already are—or find any worse way to punish me. Now we need to—"

For the second time that hour, I was cut off, this time by Noah's phone. He fished it out of his pocket with a frown. "That's my ringtone for Declan if it's something urgent."

He brought the phone to his ear. "Hey. What's going on?" Then the color drained from his face so swiftly my stomach lurched. "What?" he went on. "They really— Fuck. Okay. I— Okay. Call me back as soon as you know more."

He lowered the phone, his eyes gone dull. His throat bobbed. "Someone set the main Ashgrave residence up in flames."

*Noah*

If you only looked at the one side of the manor house, you'd have no clue that the Ashgrave home had taken any damage at all. The eastern half looked the same as it always had, the trim still perfectly white and the windows gleaming. But the western side…

Just taking it in made my stomach ball into a queasy knot. The siding and the window frames were charred black, the glass panes shattered. Holes had been eaten away in the walls. Enough of the foundation had held to keep the frame upright, which I guessed was lucky, but it was hard to feel like there was any luck involved with the destruction in front of me. A smoky tang lingered in the air, only adding to my nausea.

Next to me, Declan shifted his weight on his feet. "Thankfully, Dad was home and not near the area where the fire started. He called in our nearest friends and blacksuits for help and held off the fire on his own as well as he could until they arrived. If no one had been here to jump in right away, we'd probably have lost the whole house."

I swallowed thickly. Yes, *that* was lucky. Dad could have been so close to the fire he'd gotten caught up in it, and we might have lost both the house and our only remaining parent. There were a lot of things to be grateful for. That fact didn't stop a mix of horror and anger from searing a hole in my gut.

"Have the blacksuits confirmed the source?" I asked.

Declan grimaced. "The fire was definitely magically conjured. Regular firefighters wouldn't have been able to douse the flames. The culprits fled the scene as soon as they'd cast it—Dad didn't catch even a glimpse of them. They were careful enough not to leave any evidence behind."

I exhaled raggedly. "But it's not hard to guess who'd have had the motive."

"No. I'd be *very* surprised if this isn't an attempt by the reapers at intimidating you into backing off on investigating their spell."

I gave my brother a sharp look. "And do you think I should let myself be intimidated? You didn't really want me helping Cressida in the first place."

Declan sighed and turned to face me. "It isn't that I didn't want you to. It's that I was worried about the consequences. But you were right that it was your choice to take the risk, and that I've taken plenty in the past—for worse reasons, some of the time. I know I don't rule over *you*."

He said it so emphatically that my throat tightened even more. "Okay."

"And just to be clear, I don't blame you for what happened here. I should have thought to set up more security around the house. We'll have blacksuits patrolling regularly on all the main baron properties from now on, even if none of the barons or scions are present."

He didn't blame me, but I couldn't help feeling a little guilty all the same. The attack had happened right after we'd broken into the Warbury country property. It wasn't just an attempt at intimidating me but also a direct backlash for interfering with one of *their* homes.

I'd known I'd be putting myself in danger by throwing my lot in with Cressida, but I hadn't expected it to affect the rest of my family this much. I wasn't sure what I'd have done differently, though, other than suggest those blacksuit guards if it'd occurred to me back then.

"How quickly will they be able to reconstruct the building?" I asked. A few mages who specialized in architecture were already standing closer to the ruined wall, discussing the best approach with each other.

"It sounds like it should only take a few days. And Dad will be able to stay the whole time—his bedroom and the kitchen were untouched, and that's all he really needs."

We shared a small smile at the thought of Dad lounging at the kitchen table, savoring his morning coffee that he could often make last for a couple of hours when he was in the right contemplative mood. I glanced around. "Where is Dad?"

"The blacksuits took him to have him checked out by a doctor, just in case there are any lingering effects from the smoke or the strain of fighting the fire that weren't obvious. But he seemed fine to me. I wouldn't worry about him." Declan dragged in a breath. "You should know, though—one of the rooms that was badly hit was Mom's old study."

My pulse stuttered. My gaze shot back to the house, picking out the spot where that room would be even though its window looked out over the backyard, beyond my view. I found my mouth had gone dry.

We'd used the room that'd been specifically Mom's as a sort of memorial, with various possessions of hers on display and records Dad had thought Declan might want access to someday stashed away.

"All her stuff…" I started, and couldn't quite finish the question.

"They were able to recover a few things, but a lot of it was damaged," Declan said quietly. "You can go take a look. They say the building's stable now."

I guessed he'd already gone to survey the loss. I nodded and headed over, a tendril of grief wrapping around my stomach.

Was it harder for him or for me to have those memories stolen from us? Declan could at least remember Mom herself—although that meant he'd been able to associate the objects left behind with her more directly. He had memories of her reading the books or running a particular brush through her hair.

For me... I hadn't even been a year old when the joymancers had killed her. The contents of her room and the few photographs hung elsewhere in the house were my *only* connection to the woman who'd given birth to me. When I'd been younger, I'd sometimes hung out in her office for hours, examining one item or photo and then another, picturing the woman who should have been part of my life.

Now those fragments that'd made her real for me were gone. Because the fucking reapers had burned them away in their ridiculous desire for revenge. They were so hypocritical. Where the hell had they been when our aunt was doing whatever she could to undermine Declan?

But they only cared about loyalty to the barons who happened to share their ideals. Pricks.

My anger churned inside me as I stepped into the house and made my way down the hall, the smoky smell thickening as I went. When I reached the scorched doorway to Mom's office, the horror rose up again, blotting out everything else.

The built-in bookshelves on the far wall had crumpled in, a chunk of the lawn showing through the hole. The majority of the books that'd been on them had been reduced to cinders, singed papers scattered amid the mess. Most of the other furniture was charred too, from the leather chairs to the sleek maple desk. I could only make out blackened shapes of other objects protruding from the thinner ashes.

The side table against the wall near the door had been mostly untouched. I picked up the framed photograph that was sitting there, the glass a little heat-warped but the picture behind it still visible, and a lump rose in my throat. It showed the four of us, Mom and Dad, me and Declan, with me just a little bundled baby in Mom's arms and Declan standing tall at four years old with his hand clasped in Dad's. He'd looked awfully serious even back then.

This was what was left of our sort-of memorial: one picture, a small silver jewelry box that held one of her favorite necklaces, a toy puppy she'd conjured for Declan, an engraved pen… and a whole lot of destruction.

I stood there for several minutes, absorbing the rush of emotions. My anger came back, making my hands clench, but it felt more honed now.

We were going to take them down. We were going to show the reapers who was in charge now and that they couldn't get away with bullying their way into power anymore.

When I strode back out of the house, Declan had gone over to talk to the rebuilders. I walked over to the driveway where Cressida had parked her car next to mine. Emeric was sitting in the passenger seat with the door open to stretch his legs, watching through the windshield with an expression of sympathy. Cressida had gotten right out and was leaning against the hood, her arms folded tight over her chest.

As I came up to her, her jaw tensed. "I'm sorry," she said.

I blinked at her. "What for? This isn't your fault."

"It is, though. If I hadn't dragged you along—"

I snorted. "You hardly *dragged* me. Unless I'm remembering things very wrong, you didn't say a word about anyone coming with you, and I berated my brother —the baron—into letting me join you. I knew the reapers would probably retaliate. It's my own fault for not considering they'd do it like this."

Cressida shook her head. "It shouldn't have happened at all. My fucked-up family and their insane ideas about justice." She sucked a breath through her teeth with a hiss. "And now they've hurt you and your family too, as if you haven't gone through enough already."

"These are the consequences of being part of a barony," I said, keeping my tone light. "There are a lot of benefits that come with the position too, you know. And I highly doubt they'd have played nice even if I hadn't joined your quest. They already tried to blow all the barons up simply for existing."

Her mouth twitched, settling at a bittersweet angle. "Okay, you might have a bit of a point. But I still hate that they came after your home like this. It isn't *right*."

I squeezed her shoulder. "And that's why we're fighting them, isn't it? Because we aren't going to let them win."

"No, we're not." She met my eyes, hers flashing with more furious determination than I'd ever seen in her before. "We need to crush this rebellion and do it fast. I'm not letting them ruin anything else that matters to me."

Even as her gorgeous defiance took my breath away, my pulse hiccupped. I had a sudden image of those flames surrounding Cressida, swallowing her alive. If her parents and their allies would do this to my house, how much worse would they do to *her* given the opportunity?

Part of me wanted to tell her to back off, that we should go back to Blood U and investigate as well as we could from the relative safety there. But even as the words rose to the back of my mouth, I tamped down on them.

How could I tell her to rein in her resolve when I'd argued against Declan reining *me* in just a few days ago? She had just as much right to take those risks as I did—more, really, considering that it was her own parents involved and that her life was already in danger no matter what she did.

She didn't need me telling her to back off. She needed to know I *had* her back, every step of the way, no matter what it cost me.

Was this what leading was really about—giving the people around you the room to show their best selves rather than badgering them into fitting your preferences? It felt right.

If figuring that out was what made someone a real baron, then maybe I wouldn't be such a bad one after all.

I raised my hand to rest my fingers against her cheek. "Sounds good to me. Let's show them what happens when someone messes with Cressida Warbury."

*Cressida*

My parents might have masterminded a scheme to create a completely new type of destructive magic, but for the most part, they were pretty predictable. The chef who worked for the main Warbury estate still shopped at the same market in the same town on the same afternoon twice a week. That worked just fine for my purposes.

I checked out my reflection as I headed to the sliding glass doors that led into the upscale grocery store. The illusionary magic tingled against my skin, but not a hint of anything odd showed to the eye, even when I knew I had a spell on me. I was wearing the illusion like a costume, covering my features and figure with the appearance of the housekeeper of another nearby estate. I'd studied a few recent photographs of her for hours before attempting the casting, and I thought I'd pulled it off pretty well.

Of course, that didn't mean it'd necessarily fool someone who saw her more regularly than I did. And I was going to have to rely on a supposedly sore throat to disguise my voice, since I hadn't found any examples of that to base an illusion on. It would never hold up for more than the most casual and innocuous of conversations.

But newfound bitchiness or no, I couldn't use my own persona to get any information out of my family's staff. They'd alert my parents the second they set eyes on me.

As I stepped into the store, a waft of chilly air conditioning washed over my skin, raising goosebumps on my arms. We'd watched Nikos walk in here just five minutes ago, so I knew he was around. Drinking in the sweetly fruit-scented air, I grabbed a basket and ambled along the aisles, surreptitiously scanning for his stout form.

There. I paused at the end of the aisle he was halfway down and cleared my throat before letting out a couple of short coughs. From the corner of my eye, I saw his head come up, but I pretended I hadn't noticed him yet. I drifted down the aisle, grabbing a couple of bottles of pasta sauce off the shelf, and then glanced around.

"Nikos!" I said in my falsely hoarse voice when my gaze settled on him. "Good to see you."

He nodded. "Same to you. A little under the weather?"

I shrugged. "Nothing a little rest won't help with. Whenever the bosses give me a chance to relax." I let out a dry and equally hoarse chuckle and made a show of peeking into Nikos's basket. To my relief, there wasn't much in it, a sparse assortment of vegetables and a loaf of bread.

"Looks like the Warburys aren't working you too hard right now," I said, going for a teasing tone. "But I suppose they're away from the main house a lot these days, aren't they?"

Nikos hummed in agreement. "For the moment I only have to look after myself and a few of the staff around the house. But I'll be back in the full swing of things this weekend. There really isn't ever any resting for long." He smiled at me. "I hope you're feeling better soon."

I bobbed my head in thanks and bustled on as if I were in a hurry to finish my shopping, making a sharp turn and heading down the neighboring aisle to return to the store entrance. He'd given me exactly the information I needed—and that I'd hoped for. My parents weren't planning to be at the main residence again until the weekend. That would give us more than enough time to—

I stalled in my tracks at the end of the aisle. The *real* housekeeper I was pretending to be was walking across the parking lot toward the sliding doors.

My fingers clenched around the handle of the shopping basket, my heart stuttering. I forced myself to release the basket and set it on the floor, my mind spinning.

Shit. What were the chances?

I could manage this. I could make sure Nikos didn't see the same person again with no cold and different clothes and realize something shady was going on. I just had to work faster than I ever had in my life.

Thankfully, the chef's appearance was very fresh in my mind. I murmured several casting words with quick gestures over myself, drawing his visage over me. I'd *really* have to be careful with any talking I did while I was pretending to be a man—and watch things like how I walked too.

Cast quickly, move quickly. One of the tricks to an illusion, magical or otherwise, was never giving your audience a chance to stop and think about what they were seeing.

In my new appearance, I rushed toward the doors and burst out just as the housekeeper was reaching it. She smiled at me and raised her hand in hello. I shook my head with a scowl, motioning her back across the lot.

She frowned. "What's going on, Nikos?"

I deepened my voice into my best imitation of the chef. Him, at least, I'd known for years, so I had a decent amount of experience with his speech patterns. "Accident in the back. I almost got the stink all over me. You don't want to go in there."

Her eyes widened. "What? But I have all the shopping to do."

"Try Olivera's down the main street," I said in the same false baritone. "Half the time they've got better cuts of meat anyway." I'd heard Nikos express that sentiment more than once when I'd lived at home.

"That's true." The housekeeper sighed and gave me a briefly quizzical look. My pulse thumped faster, but I started walking away from the store as if it didn't matter to me what she did. I only let my breath out when she turned and headed back to her car.

Mission accomplished and disaster averted. That was one small victory.

My car was parked several blocks away on a secluded side street, with another illusion disguising it—and Noah's Mazda behind it—for good measure. I didn't think we could be too careful while we were this close to my parents' main stronghold.

The guys were both sitting in my car, where they'd been chatting as they waited. When I stepped past the illusion, dispelling the one on me, Emeric's expression relaxed with relief. "What did you hear?" he asked.

"We've got two days to pull this off," I said. "Unless we want to wait a while longer, which I don't think we do after the way they've started escalating. My parents won't be home until the weekend."

Noah nodded. "Perfect. But I don't suppose you can just waltz right in as if you own the place."

I grimaced. "Unfortunately, no. But I do know the habits of the staff pretty well, and I'm more familiar with the security systems there than anywhere else. My parents have no reason to assume I'd try to break onto that property—they don't know I found the mention of that book."

Emeric smiled at me. "Between the three of us, we've pulled off an awful lot. I'm sure we can manage this too. And maybe this Bernice book has the information to fill in the gaps so that we can finally get their casting off of you."

"That's the dream," I muttered. I didn't want to say

that if this part of our mission went wrong, it was almost certainly going to end with me dead. Once my parents had me at their mercy, I didn't think they'd bother toying with me anymore. I'd proven they couldn't use me, so the only thing they'd want to do with me was destroy me.

"What's the plan?" Noah asked, leaning forward eagerly. "Since we have the staff to contend with as well as magical security."

His enthusiasm brought an ache into my chest. He was so intent on helping even after his quest had nearly lost him his home—and had lost him so much that remained from his mother. I might not have ever really experienced enjoying fond ties to one's parents, but I understood that was a thing and how painful having those ties severed must be.

I wanted to tell him to go home and focus on rebuilding what the reapers had destroyed. To stop putting himself at risk over me. But I knew what he'd say. He'd already said most of it when I'd apologized to him before. I'd tried to tell him I didn't expect him to stay on after what'd happened, that it wouldn't change how I felt about him, but with typical Ashgrave stubbornness, he'd refused to listen.

Well, I guessed I wouldn't have listened to him in the same position either.

"Let's get out of town to someplace where it's less likely we'll be spotted and talk more there," I said.

He nodded and hopped out to get into his own car, where Kato had been sleeping on the dashboard. I started the Mustang's engine and spoke a few casting words to keep the illusion disguising the car glued to it as it moved. People would still *see* the car, they'd just see a different model and color—and a different woman driving it—as long as they didn't study it too closely with magically-enhanced sight.

I headed onto the main strip and down it in the opposite direction from the grocery store, wary of running into either of the people whose faces I'd put on today again. I'd just stopped at a red light when Emeric stiffened in his seat.

"What?" I said, but when I followed his gaze, I no longer needed his answer.

Ernest and Harriet Mismeren were sitting with another couple and a single, older man at a patio table outside a restaurant about half a block beyond the lights, peering at the people and cars passing by. The hairs lifted on the back of my neck.

I flicked on my signal, knowing Noah would follow my lead even if he didn't know why. It felt too risky to drive right past them.

"What do you think they're doing here?" I asked Emeric as I made the turn, pitching my voice low instinctively as if they'd be able to hear me all the way over there. The blacksuits had arrested the Achelings and the Haythorpes for our kidnapping, but the Mismerens hadn't been directly involved in that part of the plot, so they'd escaped that harsh a punishment.

Emeric's mouth had flattened. "My best guess would be that they're still trying to curry favor with the higher families. They might even be keeping a lookout specifically for us."

Damn it. As if we needed more complications. I gritted my teeth and continued down the side-street until I could make another turn.

When I finally parked on a sheltered country lane a couple of miles outside of town, my stomach had tied itself into several knots. Noah got out next to us, his expression already concerned. "What happened back there with the sudden turn?"

"We spotted a bunch of reapers staked out on the main street," Emeric answered for me. "One of the main Portland families and a few others. I'd bet a lot of the lower families have picked spots near the main residences of the higher powers so they'll be in place if there's a chance to jump in and help."

"Bastards," I muttered, and sighed. "Maybe they'll stay in town, but this means we have to be prepared that they might take up watch around my parents' house when we want to get in there too. And exactly when it'd otherwise be easiest for us to sneak in—at night, when everyone except a couple of guards will be sleeping."

"So we deal with them too," Noah said. "They aren't the most powerful mages around, or they wouldn't need to be hanging around trying to offer favors, right?"

"They could still make quite a bit of trouble." Emeric swiped his hand over his mouth. "But I may be able to help with that. They'll be more pissed off with me than with anyone else. If they come at us, I can get them to focus on me."

My heart stuttered all over again. "I don't want you drawing their attention."

He met my gaze. "If that's the easiest way to give you a clear path to getting your answers, I'm happy to do it." He offered me a crooked smile. "Anyway, maybe I'd kind of like the chance to tangle with them again and show I'm not the useless cripple they saw me as."

I didn't know what to say to that. My gaze slid to Noah. He reached out and clasped my hand, and I knew there was no point in arguing. It was either get on with this or give up… and I'd decided giving up wasn't my thing weeks ago.

"Okay," I said. "Let's figure out that plan—one that should mean *none* of us ends up in the line of fire if we work it right."

*Emeric*

Apprehension wound around my stomach as we drove along the highway toward the private lane that led to the main Warbury residence. It was one thing to break into an out-of-the-way property that the Warburys rarely used and didn't have as much stake in protecting. But their primary home—I couldn't imagine how much more brutal the spells defending it might be.

On the other hand, Cressida had spent a lot more of her life there, so she'd at least be more familiar with the quirks and weak spots. That should work to our advantage.

And if we didn't try this, we had no other major leads to follow up on.

It was well into night, the clouds overhead blotting out most of the stars. Only thin moonlight streamed down over the road from a half-concealed moon that was just a sliver shy of full. The road was eerily silent. We hadn't passed any traffic in half an hour.

Cressida drew in a shaky breath and glanced at Noah's car behind us through the rearview mirror. Her hands flexed on the steering wheel.

"I hope I can manage to circumvent the main security system completely," she said. "It's not even unusual to have a secret passage built onto the property—a lot of the major families have ways of getting in and out of the main building if there's some kind of trouble. My parents don't know that I'm aware of where ours is. My grandmother showed me when I was little because she thought it'd be good for me to know." She paused, her mouth twisting. "I wonder if that was her way of trying to protect me. If she could tell I wasn't really going to be safe in that house, but she didn't know what else to do about it."

My heart ached for her. I didn't know what to say, so what came out was an attempt at lightening the mood. "And here you are using it to get back into the house instead of out of it."

My effort landed well—Cressida's lips twitched into a small smile. "True. If they haven't gone and changed the outside access point or ramped up the spells protecting *that* more than I'd expect. It should be mostly illusions to stop anyone from realizing it's there in the first place. They never thought I'd get very far with illusionary magic as my only real strength, but it might end up saving my life and the baronies."

"I think you've already proven several times over that they horribly underestimated you," I said. Then my gaze caught on a tiny, shadowy shape in the distance, and my nerves prickled. I reached out and touched Cressida's arm. "Stop at the side of the road."

Cressida frowned, but she did as I asked. Noah pulled over behind us and waited for our next cue. Thankfully, we'd been driving with the headlights off since we'd left any significant civilization behind. I didn't think anyone that far ahead would have spotted us, at least not clearly.

"What is it?" Cressida asked.

I motioned to the shape I'd seen. A moment later, the clouds pulled farther back from the moon, and the brighter beams glinted off the polished metal frame of a sedan parked on the shoulder like we now were, about a mile away. "You see the car? Is that where the private drive to the estate is?"

Cressida's eyes widened. "I can't see the actual drive from here, but it's about the right distance. And there's no good reason for someone to be hanging around at the entrance." She muttered a curse under her breath. "It'll be the reapers we saw earlier, I guess?"

"They're the only ones who'd think they have a good reason. I'd be willing to bet that's the Mismerens and maybe their friends too, staking out the place like some kind of volunteer guards." I grimaced. "I'm sure they'll be scanning for magic, so we can't slip past them using an illusion—if they've even left room to drive past them. Is there another way to get to the property without getting near them?"

Cressida sucked her lower lip under her teeth as her gaze turned pensive. "Not by car. But then we couldn't have risked driving the whole way to the front gate anyway. I was counting on the cars at least getting us closer, though. It's still another ten miles down the private road. It'd be quite a hike covering all that distance from here."

I glanced over the landscape around us, nearly flat fields with nothing more than shaggy clumps of grass and tufts of wildflowers on most of the terrain. "And there isn't any cover. Unless we crawl the whole way, all they'd have to do is glance in the right direction and they might see us."

"Yeah." Cressida's brow had knit. "I should talk to Noah and see if he has any ideas."

The ache that had formed in my chest earlier tightened into a noose. It was my fault those jackasses were out here in the first place—my fault they'd ever targeted Cressida, my fault they were pissed off at both of us enough to think it was worth hanging around running surveillance just in case they got the chance to play heroes for the higher reaper families. *I* should be the one dealing with them.

I'd intended to be the one who did when we first saw them, but driving right up to them and confronting them didn't seem like the wisest approach.

An idea wound through my mind, risky but only for me. "Hold on," I said to Cressida. "That secret entrance— you said it's mostly protected by illusions? You're not likely to need a ton of physicality skill to get past it?"

"I think I'll probably have to tackle it on my own either way," Cressida said. "The defenses around here will be even more highly tuned to reject magic from anyone who's not a Warbury. But—" She stopped and studied me, a shadow crossing her face. "What are you thinking of doing that means you wouldn't be there with me anyway?"

I motioned to the car in the distance. "Like I said before, they're probably way more pissed off with me than anyone else, including you. It'd make your job a hell of a lot easier if I redirected their attention, wouldn't it? Lead them on a chase after me and clear the road so you and Noah can go on your way."

I could see the argument in Cressida's expression before she spoke. "I can't let you go off like some kind of bait to draw them away—what will they do to you if they catch up with you?"

"Nothing good," I acknowledged, "so I just won't let them catch me." I held up my titanium hand. "They already see me as a weakling and a cripple. It's easier to keep ahead of people who're underestimating you. And you wouldn't be leaving me totally adrift. I think I'd need to borrow your car to make this work."

I wasn't over-confident enough to think I could outpace the other reapers on foot. Besides, I'd want to get them as far from the Warbury estate and Cressida as I could.

Cressida let out a breath with a noise of frustration and fixed me with a firm look. "Are you completely sure about this? Because I'd never ask you to."

I smiled at her, my spirits truly lifting for maybe the first time since I'd recognized the awful spell the reapers had cast onto her. "And that's why I'm happy to do it for you. For all of us. I'll be safer too if we can get this spell off of you. My sister will be. I want to help you, but it isn't totally selfless. So you're not allowed to feel guilty about it."

A sputter of a laugh escaped Cressida's mouth. "Fuck. Fine, if you insist. And do whatever you have to do to keep yourself safe. I don't care what happens to the car. I can buy another of those."

She leaned over to give me a quick but intense kiss, enough to make my pulse thump even as she pulled back. Oh, yes, whatever happened, it'd be worth it to know I'd done my best for this woman.

We both got out, and Noah did too. Cressida went to him as I came around to the driver's side, where she'd left the fob in the ignition.

"The reapers we saw in town today are staked out by the entrance to the private road like I was afraid they might be," she told the Ashgrave scion before he had to ask. "Emeric's going to divert them in my car. The rest will be up to the two of us."

Noah gave me an assessing look, and it warmed me a little to recognize the worry in his eyes—worry for me, not about whether I could be counted on.

What we had with Cressida was more than just sharing a woman we both cared about, wasn't it? We'd become our own close-knit unit of three, all of us looking out for each other.

It wasn't the kind of relationship I'd ever imagined for myself, but now that I had it, I couldn't picture anything better.

"I guess I don't need to tell you to be careful," Noah

said. "You know what those pricks are like better than we do. But by order of a scion, I do expect to see you back at the hotel by tomorrow morning."

My lips curled with a crooked grin at the wryness in his tone. "Duly noted." I turned to Cressida and couldn't resist taking the moment to step closer to her again. I bowed my head over hers, our foreheads almost brushing, and touched her cheek. I hadn't said the words out loud before, but if there ever was a moment, it was now. "I love you. No matter what happens, that'll still be true."

She swallowed audibly, gazing up at me with a liquid shimmer in her eyes. "I love you too. Let's show the reapers what we're *all* made of. And that they shouldn't mess with anyone who's partly made out of titanium."

I outright laughed at that before giving her another kiss, my heart swelling at the returned confession. Then I got into the car, not wanting to linger any longer in case the reapers noticed us all the way down here and wondered what was going on.

Maybe it isn't the reapers at all, I thought to myself as I snapped on my seatbelt and started the engine. Maybe we've made a fuss over nothing and it's some random kids making out on the side of the road.

That would have been nice, but as I drove on down the road and the sedan came more clearly into view, I recognized it as the Mismerens'. I'd seen that old BMW parked at various social events for years.

There was no way we could have gotten around them unnoticed. They'd parked right across the entrance to the drive, obviously assuming no one would be heading toward the Warbury property at this time of night unless they had illicit intentions. My jaw clenched.

Part of me wanted to roar right up to them and give them a piece of my mind. But as satisfying as that might feel, it'd probably get me killed and not help Cressida at all. Like I'd told her, they saw me as weak—as a useless coward who'd backed down when we'd almost achieved victory.

That was fine. I didn't care what they thought anymore. If their assumption helped me get the victory I actually wanted now, it was even good.

I slowed a little as I got closer as if I'd just noticed them and was deciding what to do. Abruptly, a conjured light flared between us, shining through my windshield. I couldn't see them yet, but no doubt they'd identified me.

So I did what they'd figure a coward like me would do.

I let my face twitch with surprise and fear that wasn't totally faked, since I was in danger. They'd get a taste of that fear to convince them. Then I rammed my foot on the gas and tore past them down the road as if I were terrified of what would happen if they caught me.

The growl of the engine behind me told me they'd taken the bait. I pushed the pedal down harder, grateful for the excellent engine in this piece of fine machinery, knowing the reapers were almost definitely already hurling spells my way in an attempt to disable the car. I turned on the headlights, both wanting them to be able to stay on my tail and needing to see so I didn't take myself right off the road. And in the back of my mind, another plan started to form.

They'd be hurling spells at me… so why couldn't I leave one waiting for them? It obviously hadn't even occurred to them that they might have to worry about me fighting back.

Spurred on by the thud of my heart, I started intoning casting words into the stillness of the car. One piece and then another and another, keeping the effect small so I didn't have to plant it anywhere yet, seeing the construct I was building in my mind's eye.

This was what I was meant for: creating things, not destroying them. And if my creation could stop these assholes from carrying out their own destruction, so much the better.

When we'd put a couple dozen miles between us and the road to the Warbury residence, I eased on the gas just a little to make myself an even more tempting target. The car behind me seemed to roar louder as if lunging at me as I supposedly faltered.

Then I flung my spell onto the road behind me with a few snapped syllables to stretch it out across the entire strip of pavement.

I only got to glimpse the effect in the rearview mirror as I continued racing away, but the sound was satisfying enough. The BMW sped along the road—and smacked straight into the trap I'd conjured.

The engine blew with a sputtered popping sound. All four tires burst in a tight series of bangs. The doors crumpled inward, not enough to crush anyone, but mangled enough to make them impossible to open without a whole lot of effort. And as a cherry on top, the little intricate casting I'd layered over the larger effects would have shattered the inner workings of any phones in the vehicle, making it impossible for them to call for help.

They'd force their way out eventually and trudge to the nearest town, but we'd all be long gone by then.

Assuming Cressida didn't run into an even worse problem back at her former home.

*Cressida*

The entrance of the Warbury secret escape passage was exactly where my grandmother had shown me fifteen years ago. The only way I found it was because I knew to look for it. Noah had walked right past it a few seconds before without any idea.

I made a soft noise to call him back and circled the spot where I could sense the magic. It was a small cluster of trees, one of several copses scattered around the fields near the tall stone wall that surrounded the Warbury residence. But I happened to know that the tree directly in the center wasn't a tree at all, only an illusion of one disguising an entrance underneath.

In the distance, Percy sent a brief impression of curiosity. It bugged my familiar that I'd told him to keep his distance for tonight's operation, but we couldn't risk the possibility that someone would spot him and realize I was around. I thought an impression of chilling out and letting me handle this back at him. Then I eased between two of the outer trees to study the illusionary one more closely.

The conjuring was powerful magic, every ridge in the bark perfectly shaped. Even knowing that it wasn't real, my mind couldn't quite accept that fact. Even when I rested my fingers against it, the spell sent the impression of a rough, cool surface into my skin.

"It's here?" Noah whispered.

I nodded and ran my tongue over my teeth. I couldn't sense any strong protective spells in the area. For my purposes, the convenient thing about an illusion-based defense was that the casters couldn't afford to expend a lot of other magic in the same area, or it'd be too easy for someone searching to pick up on the additional energy and figure out there was something important about this spot.

Of course, even with strong illusionary powers, I couldn't just dispel this conjured image. Removing it completely might set off a warning alert anyway. I cocked my head and spoke a few tentative casting words to get a deeper feel for the magic.

There were layers upon layers, from different Warburys adding to the effect over the decades. If I'd stuck with my parents, they might have told me about this passage when I'd graduated, and I'd have been adding my own magic to bolster the disguise in just a few months. The thought of that alternate reality made me a little queasy.

"I don't want to destroy the spell," I murmured to

Noah. "I just need to open it up a little, move the illusion around so we can squeeze through it. I think if I just…"

I narrowed my eyes with concentration and intoned another casting word and then several more. Gradually, carefully, the base of the trunk split open, bark and roots moving outward on either side, a gap opening in the middle. All I could see right now beneath the tree was loamy soil, but when I cast the same parting effect on that area…

The dirt swept aside, and a stone staircase swam into view where it had been.

Noah let out a hushed chuckle. "That's really something. The Warburys honestly thought they might have to use this someday to make a quick escape?"

I shrugged. "I guess there was a lot more infighting between the fearmancer families a century or more ago. We didn't like the idea of being potentially cornered in our own home. And even now—they're toeing the line of obvious treason on a regular basis. I bet they'd appreciate this option if the blacksuits came calling with an arrest warrant."

"Hmm," Noah said. "Good to keep in mind."

I eased down the steps first, into a passage that was only a little taller than I was, lined with more worn stones. When Noah reached the bottom of the stairs, he had to keep his head ducked to avoid bumping it on the ceiling. The air was even chillier down there, thick with an earthy scent that filled my noise and gave me the vague impression of suffocating.

I dragged in a long breath to prove to myself that my

lungs still worked just fine and set off down the passage. Noah padded along behind me.

"Where will it let us out?" he asked, still keeping his voice very low.

"The back of the wine cellar," I said. "We'll just have to keep an eye out for staff once we're there. My parents usually have at least two guards patrolling the grounds here and one inside the house even when they're not home." And it was possible they'd increased that security since the conflict with the new barons had started coming to a head.

It felt like we'd walked at least a mile when the passage ended with a solid oak door. I grazed my fingers along its edge, feeling the magic laced along it, and spoke a few words. To my relief, it swung open at my nudge.

We emerged into a sheltered corner of the wine cellar, unable to see anything but the racks of bottles directly in front of us. When I shut the door behind us, an illusion on it blended it perfectly into the rest of the plaster wall. I stared at it for a long moment to commit the exact position to my memory.

Turning to Noah, I cast an illusion over both of us that wouldn't hold up to close scrutiny if we were moving but would help us blend into the shadows, and then slunk past the racks toward the doorway.

The basement was as still and silent as ever, but the faint sound of footsteps filtered through from the floor above us. My pulse skittered even though the guard was nowhere near us yet.

The book would be in the library, which was on the

second floor. We had to get all the way up there without being spotted.

Noah followed close behind me as I crept to the stairs that led to the first floor. At the top of the steps, I peered out into the darkened kitchen. My eyes had adjusted to the darkness, and I could tell no one was moving between the island and the glossy countertops. I couldn't hear the guard's footsteps anymore, though, so I had no idea where he was now.

We slipped down the hall, keeping close to the wall and setting our feet as softly as we could. The grand mahogany staircase came into view up ahead in the dim light that filtered from the outer security lamps through the windows next to the front doors. My heart started to lift, but just as I'd taken another step toward the staircase, the guard strode into view.

He passed the hall with only a quick glance our way, my illusion hiding us well enough to avoid his notice. But he stopped just out of view at the other side of the foyer with a tap of his shoes. He stood there for a minute and then walked back past the staircase again. As we watched, the same pattern repeated again.

They'd ordered him to focus on the front door, I realized. Maybe there were other guards in other key rooms on the ground level that could serve as entry points, and they hadn't wanted to risk having them moving around so much that an intruder could work around them.

My heart thumped faster, my mouth going dry as I pondered how the hell we were going to get past him. My illusion wouldn't be good enough to disguise us in the clearer light of the foyer, especially while we were in motion.

And every second we lingered here, we risked another guard catching us from behind.

I debated crafting an illusion to distract the guard, something that would catch his eye in an adjoining room —but as soon as he realized what it was, he'd know someone was in the house and launch a full search. My stomach knotted. Had we come this far only to get stuck so close to our goal?

Noah touched my arm. He leaned close to my ear, his voice barely more than a breath. "Can you make an illusion that looks like you?"

My head jerked around. "What?" I whispered.

"Make an illusion of you. Just good enough to hold up in the dark at a distance. I can take a page from Emeric's book, make a run for it, and distract the guard, but I don't want him worrying about you being somewhere else in the house. If he thinks he's chasing both of us, you'll be in the clear."

His logic made sense, but my chest clenched up anyway. It'd been bad enough letting Emeric race off to face danger alone on my behalf. Now Noah too?

But we were running out of time. I didn't have any better ideas. I nodded and started murmuring under my breath, drawing an image like a reflection of me into being between us. In a couple of minutes, a slightly blurred but reasonably convincing version of me stood motionless by the wall. With a little more spellwork, I tied the illusion's movements to Noah's, so it'd echo the motions of his limbs—just not so perfectly that the copying would be obvious.

"Make for the back wall," I said. "The protections are designed to stop people from getting in, not to keep them from getting out—you should be able to get over it no problem. There's a thicker patch of forest beyond the wall that you'll have an easier time dodging them in if the guards follow you that far."

Noah nodded and leaned in to brush a kiss to my lips. Then he slunk forward, the illusion of me trailing behind him. As I watched, my hands balled at my sides.

Noah waited until the guard had walked to the far end of the room. Just as the man turned, he leapt as if to make a dash up the stairs.

The guard shouted and swung the rest of the way around. Noah let out a yelp and sprinted for the neighboring room instead—away from me. The illusion of me darted after him, and the guard charged off in pursuit.

I longed to throw a spell after him to slow him down, but that would only blow my cover. Willing down the protective urge inside me, I hurried to the stairs and scrambled up them.

Not a moment too soon. The guard's shouts rang out, and another man hustled by through the foyer, not even glancing at the spot where I froze by the top of the stairs. I waited until he was gone and darted across the upper hall to the library.

The second the door clicked shut behind me, I exhaled

in relief, but I wasn't anywhere near safe yet. I rushed over to the shelves of rare books my parents treasured so much.

It was still here, wasn't it? They never took the precious volumes outside the library for fear any disturbance would damage the fragile ancient pages.

Bernice, Bernice, Bernice… My skimming finger stopped on the worn leather spine stamped with the words *Bernice Havercoil's Insights in Twisted Specialties.*

I tugged the book out and set it on one of the side tables by the room's various upholstered chairs. The pages fanned open, giving off a musty smell, and settled on a spot where someone had wedged in a folded page of much newer paper.

I unfolded the paper and peered at the tiny notations and diagrams marked on it. It only took a few seconds for me to recognize the sorts of patterns and combination of spells that must have gone into the magic cast onto me. My heart leapt.

It wasn't a complete diagram by any means, but this was proof that my parents had been instrumental in creating that spell. A spell that had been used to attack a scion and, through me, to target the barons. If the blacksuits couldn't arrest them over that, I didn't know what would do it.

I snapped a couple of pictures of the paper using my phone with its flash and then of the pages of Bernice's book where it'd been wedged. With a few flicks of my thumb, I sent the images to the barons and to the blacksuit contact I'd been given when I left campus, explaining where I'd found them. Probably no one would look at the photos until the morning, but I didn't want to risk them not seeing this at all.

Only then did I take a good look at the book for myself. My gaze skimmed over the lines of text, and something inside me went very still. I turned the page, and then another, my lips parting as the information sunk in.

This chapter was focused on using a target's own mental state to add qualities to a spell. There was a whole section on the possibility of using someone's lack of awareness of a casting to conceal the magic. It'd only been a theory, but it seemed like it'd worked. As long as I'd had no idea anyone had worked magic on me, the spell had appeared to not exist. Freaky.

But now that I knew it existed, they couldn't hide it anymore. And that wasn't even the main part I found interesting. Deeper into the chapter, Bernice mentioned that she suspected that tying a spell to a target's mental state could have one obvious downside. As soon as the victim realized what you'd done, they would be able to use their mind to manipulate the spell too. Maybe with extreme difficulty, but you couldn't stop them from working on it if you'd already tied it to their thoughts.

*Depending on the spell, a target's interference might work something like peeling back the layers of the casting to remove it completely—or pressing those layers in on themselves to trigger a particular effect. Either result is possible. For this reason, I recommend only experimenting with this type of approach with spells that would be set off swiftly after activation, before the target has time to understand their situation.*

I took a picture of that page too, a giddy shiver racing down the center of me. If her assumptions were correct… then I might be able to unravel the spell myself. I'd never even tried because it'd sounded so far outside my abilities, when several experts hadn't managed it and when the consequences of failure had been so huge. My parents had probably counted on me never suspecting I could control it myself.

Well, actually, they'd probably counted on me being blown up into tiny pieces before I had a chance to even think about it.

I briefly debated taking the entire book with me and then decided I needed to leave it here as evidence. I was just straightening my posture when the library door swung open, and Mom and Dad stalked into the room.

*Cressida*

I had no time to cast a spell or dive for a hiding place. Mom and Dad had clearly come in expecting to find me here. Their gazes shot straight to me and to the book beneath my hand.

It was Bernice who saved me. They couldn't bear to risk damaging anything in their precious collection. So instead of blasting me away right there, Mom cast a more muted spell that simply knocked me to the side onto the floor.

My hand was still clenched around my phone. Instinctively, I hit the call button for whichever contact I'd last texted. As my shoulder smacked into the floor, I let the impact jolt the phone from my fingers. It slid under a chair.

I shoved myself behind the same piece of furniture, just as another bolt of magic careened toward me, this one more vicious than the last. It tore a chunk of upholstery off the side of the chair.

"Stop!" I shouted—on the slim chance that whoever I'd called had picked up and would hear to realize I needed help, not because I expected my parents to listen to me. "Don't hurt me!"

"It's a little late for making requests like that, isn't it, Cressida?" my mother said in a darkly sneering voice.

Their footsteps were already whispering across the floor toward me. I didn't know how they'd known to come back to the house or how they'd gotten here so quickly. Had I screwed up in town with Nikos, and he'd tipped them off that something suspicious was going on? Had they fed him a false story to begin with and actually been lurking around here the whole time, guessing that I might come?

I had no idea, and it didn't really matter. All that mattered was that it was game over—for me, at least. In a matter of seconds, they'd kill me.

It wouldn't be a total victory for them, though. I'd sent enough information to the barons that hopefully they'd be able to dispel any future iterations of this new type of casting. My parents and their reaper friends wouldn't be able to use it in their rebellion anymore. Maybe the blacksuits would even be able to make some arrests.

But that wasn't enough. As I braced myself behind the chair, a surge of defiance swept through me.

I didn't want to die. I was only just figuring out how good *living* could be. And I sure as hell didn't want to let my parents ruin my life even more than they already had. They didn't call the shots any longer.

But what could I do? There was nothing around that I could defend myself with, and no one close enough to help me unless I managed to hold Mom and Dad off for at least a little while. I didn't have any spells I could cast well enough to challenge their magical abilities other than illusions, and what good was an illusion when—

Professor Burnbuck's voice rose up in the back of my head. *Be a woman the reapers and your parents can't touch, even if you're shaken inside… and you'll be much closer to having that be true.* The words I'd read in the Bernice book raced through my mind in a whirl, and the idea clicked into place in my head.

"You don't want to get any closer," I said in the best bitchy voice I could summon, all chill and menace. "Unless you're looking to get blown up too."

The footsteps paused. They were only a few paces from the chair now, but they'd stopped moving. That was a small win in itself.

"What are you talking about?" my father said, and scoffed. "You don't have that kind of physicality power. Do you think we're not shielded?"

"Maybe enough to protect you against anything I could produce by myself," I retorted. "But what about your own magic? Can you make a shield strong enough that the spell you intended to slaughter the barons with won't break it?"

Their momentary silence told me I was on the right track. They weren't laughing off the idea that I could manipulate their spell to my own ends. They knew what book I'd been looking at, the information I must have seen.

Of course, I had no freaking clue how I would actually go about triggering the explosive part of the spell embedded in my tooth. I didn't really want to trigger it, because *I* didn't want to explode. But they didn't know any of that. As long as they saw a desperate girl holding on to the one piece of power she still had, a girl who hadn't hesitated to turn against them in the past, I could make them believe.

An illusion without a single bit of magic.

They weren't that easily persuaded right off the bat, but then, I hadn't expected them to be. My mother raised her voice again, her tone still sharp but more careful than before. "You have no idea how a spell that intricate works. You could never manage to control it yourself."

I snorted. "How many experts do you think I had studying me and talking about how the casting must have been done? How poor do you think my magical theory is? I might not be a wunderkind, but you've heard my performance reports from school: I'm no slouch either. All I needed was the tip-off that the reins were really in my hands."

"Big words from a frightened little child," Dad muttered, and his shoe squeaked against the floor with another step.

It was time to add some actual magic to the illusion—and hope like hell that someone would get here with backup before my parents totally called my bluff. I murmured a casting so faint they had no chance of hearing it and pushed myself onto my feet behind the chair.

An eerie glow had lit up all over my skin. Or rather, *inside* my skin, flickering and churning as if I'd activated some kind of fiery energy within my body. I'd kept it toned down for now, but even so, it was bright enough in the dark room to cast a ruddy glaze on the shelves around me—and my parents' staring faces.

"Just a little more, and it'll destroy you, me, and most of the house too," I said, holding Mom's gaze and then Dad's unwaveringly. "You did this to me, and I'm not going down without taking you with me."

Dad halted again, even backing up a step so he returned to where he must have been standing before next to Mom. My mother wet her lips. Her eyes were still narrowed, but a gleam had come into them that looked more like fear than anger. A giddy tingle of that energy traveled into the store of magic behind my breastbone, confirming my impression. More flowed into me from Dad.

I'd made my parents *afraid*. After all the terror they'd provoked in me over the years, the thought seemed impossible, but there it was.

I pushed my advantage, drawing in a breath around a hushed casting word, urging the illusionary fire beneath my skin to glow a tad more fiercely. I couldn't rush it, couldn't take the effect to its limit too quickly, or they'd realize I wasn't actually going to explode. The more time I bought myself, the more chance I'd survive this standoff.

A momentary hopelessness wove through my resolve. *Would* anyone come? Would they risk breaking into a major fearmancer family's home just to save me?

But that doubt only pricked at me for an instant. I knew it was wrong. I had friends. I had two men who loved me. I had rulers who respected what I could do for the community. *Someone* would come—as soon as they knew I needed them, as fast as they could get here. I'd somehow earned that kind of loyalty along the road that'd led me here.

I just needed to hold on for long enough to give them the chance.

I groped for some other way to keep my parents engaged in the confrontation. "It doesn't have to end like this," I said, keeping up my mean girl persona. "You *do* have a choice here. Let me walk away, and you won't end up in tiny pieces all over your precious library."

Dad grimaced. "And have you go running off to your traitor friends and the false barons they worship? I don't think so. But maybe we could find some other sort of compro—"

I caught the twitch of Mom's fingers, the parting of her lips, and made the glow inside me flare so bright another jolt of fear rushed from them into me. "Don't even try to sneak in a casting," I snapped at them. "I'm holding on tight to the last bit of pressure this spell needs to detonate. If I see anything from either of you, I can set it off in an instant."

Mom's hand stilled. "It didn't have to be like this," she said stiffly. "If you'd stood by us, upheld the principles every fearmancer should—we didn't *want* to use you this way. You gave us no choice."

I snorted. "If I'd stood by you, you'd have kept stomping me down under your heels every chance you got. You never gave me a chance to do anything *other* than be used by you. You're just bothered that you lost a tool you thought you'd get to have so much more control over. Just because you gave birth to me doesn't mean you *own* me. I only wish it hadn't taken me so long to figure that out."

Dad drew himself up haughtily. "You can't pretend we didn't take care of you. You had everything you could have wanted and more. More than most of the mages you've allied yourself with now do. Even—"

"No," I broke in with another flare. The illusion was starting to sting my own eyes. I must look like a girl made out of light to them. I wouldn't be able to push it much farther. But talking—talking was keeping them distracted from whether I would actually go through with my threat.

"Do you think the clothes and the car and all that really mattered?" I demanded. "I'd have traded all that in a snap for parents who actually cared that the prick they hired to tutor me was raping me on a regular basis. Who didn't see even the worst pain I went through in my life as something to celebrate because of how it was hardening me up or bending me to their will. If there's one thing we're going to get straight before we all die here, it's that you were absolutely shitty parents. I've never regretted getting away from you."

I couldn't tell from my parents' expressions whether

my announcement had affected them at all. Mom looked more annoyed than anything else. But I found I didn't care whether my feelings made any difference to them. I'd said my truth, and they'd heard it, and that was enough, no matter what they made of it.

It was my life now, not theirs, even if it ended here by their hands. At least I'd managed to figure that out before I went.

Dad was eyeing me with an analytical air that made my skin twitch. Was he realizing that I was only putting on a show, not really controlling their spell at all? "Let's just get this over with, then," he growled, and marched toward me.

My heart stuttered. I reached deep inside me, focusing on the tooth that had been the center of so much of my agony over the past few weeks, thinking maybe I could figure out how to trigger it after all—

The window at the far end of the room shattered. The library door burst open. Blacksuits stormed into the room, hurling out castings before their feet had even hit the floor.

As spells whipped around my parents, paralyzing them, another blacksuit grabbed me and yanked me farther away from them. The others closed in around Mom and Dad.

"You're under arrest by the order of the barons on a long list of charges," the leader announced, glowering down at my parents, and my chest sagged with an exhaled breath of relief. I let go of the illusion I'd cast through my body, and the glow flickered out.

"Are you all right, Miss Warbury?" the blacksuit who'd caught me asked.

I nodded, my thoughts already leaping to the people not in the room. "Noah Ashgrave—and Emeric—are they—"

She gave my shoulder a reassuring pat before I'd even gotten the question out. "They're just fine. Giving evidence to my colleagues right now."

I let out another breath, and a fractured laugh came with it. In that case, I really was all right—as all right as I could ever remember being in my entire life.

*Cressida*

*Five months later*

I spoke one more casting word to deepen the hue on my client's lips and then stepped back to take in the full effect of the illusions I'd painted across her face. After my most recent adjustments, they added a subtle enhancement to her eyes, mouth, and cheeks similar to Nary-style make-up. It looked like I'd gotten the balance just right.

"All you have to do is activate it with a casting word," I said with a smile, "and you'll get the full magical effect. Only in mage company, of course. Why don't you give it a try?"

The woman peered at the mirror and murmured under

her breath. In an instant, the sheen of color decorating her eyelids started to sparkle at the corners of her eyes, just as she'd asked for. The faint ruddy shade on her cheekbones wound into her dark hair, turning into a deeper hue as it went, until it looked like red streamers were mingling with the locks.

It wasn't a style I'd have gone for myself, but she gasped and grinned like I'd given her the best birthday gift she'd ever received. "It's perfect. Wow! I can't wait to show it off."

"And it'll hold at least a month," I said. "My illusions have great staying power. If you want them touched up after a few weeks or adjusted in any way, just book another appointment."

"I'll definitely be doing that," she said. When she paid at the register, she left me a tip so big it was embarrassing, especially because I wasn't hurting for cash.

I knew what Noah would say if I mentioned that to him. *It's a testament to your talent, mon petit chou-fleur.* I was starting to learn to take my clients' generosity that way.

Magical makeup wasn't a line of work I'd imagined getting into in general when I'd pictured my life after I graduated from Blood U. Mostly because I'd told myself I'd put my superficial days behind me. But sometime during all the trials I'd been through since taking up the mission against the reapers in Portland, I'd started to appreciate the value of choosing what kind of face you offered to the world a lot more.

It wasn't really superficial. There were all kinds of

elements of confidence and freedom that came into it as well. And I *was* good at this kind of work. Maybe I'd branch out into other areas of illusionary magic later on, but since I'd joined the salon shortly after graduation, my skills had come into high demand. It felt pretty amazing to be able to offer something that so many of my fellow mages were eager to accept, that they didn't feel they could pull off on their own.

The woman with the sparkly eyes had been my last client for the day. I closed up the salon with a wave to the owner, who shot me a thumbs-up. Percy stirred where he'd been perched on a nearby rooftop between periods of cruising around in the sky and lifted off to follow me. I headed down the street to meet Emeric.

He'd ended up getting work with a company that specialized in making magically enhanced prosthetics like his own and assistive conducting pieces like the one Jude Killbrook used to supplement his ability to store energy. Their main office was just a short walk from the salon. We'd been carpooling to a parking garage about halfway in between the two businesses.

He was already at the car when I reached it, leaning against the Mustang's hood and reading over something on his phone. At the sound of my footsteps, he glanced up and put the device away, his gaze traveling over me with an appreciative gleam I didn't think I'd ever get tired of. "Good day?"

"Very good," I said, sliding into the driver's seat. "You?"

He got in next to me. "Today I took the lead on

making a piece that let a guy who hasn't worked any magic in three years finally cast a spell again. Hard to think of anything much better than that."

I laughed as I started the engine. "Okay, that doesn't really compare to decorating people's faces."

He shrugged. "Different kinds of people, different kinds of healing. I think you've more than proven how much of an impact an illusion can make."

"True." My tongue flicked to press against the tooth I'd pretended I was going to detonate to hold off my parents' attack. With the additional magical theory from the spellbooks the blacksuits had confiscated as evidence, the experts who'd been working on my case had been able to coach me through removing the reaper's casting through much more real means. It hadn't ached or sent me off on any murderous missions since then, a fact I was incredibly grateful for.

I had a lot to be grateful for these days, really. I even liked the drive to and from work as much as the work itself. The companionable conversation and occasional silences with Emeric. The knowledge that we were going home together—to the first place I'd had that really *was* my home.

And not just mine and Emeric's. About half an hour after we'd gotten back to our apartment, Noah strode in, back from Blood U for the weekend. "There's been another arrest," he announced cheerfully without preamble. Kato chittered with equal enthusiasm and leapt from the Ashgrave scion's shoulder onto the side table.

My eyebrows rose. Once the blacksuits had gotten

their hands on my parents with enough evidence to incarcerate them, the other reaper families had started to fall like dominos. I'd thought just about all of them had already ended up in the fearmancer prison or under enforced house arrest by now.

"Who?" I asked.

"One of the smaller families in Portland that it just took a while to find enough evidence on," Noah said, tipping his head to Emeric. "The Kiverdells?"

Emeric nodded. "Right, they tended to lurk around the sidelines whenever the others were plotting anything. I'm not surprised it took a while to nab them."

I leaned back on the leather sofa, stretching my legs onto the ottoman. "That's got to be just about everyone now, right? The rebellion is totally quashed?"

Noah flopped down next to me and slipped his arm around mine. "I'm sure there are a few stragglers—and there are a bunch of prominent families whose loyalties are up in the air but who didn't get actively involved in any plots. We might see some minor rebellions in the future. It'll definitely be very hard for them to strike any significant blows at this point, though."

I beamed at him. "That's good enough for me. Especially since you're going to be full baron in less than a year now. One less reason for me to be totally terrified by that possibility."

He waggled his eyebrows at me. "Oh, I can be very terrifying if I want to be."

I giggled, and Emeric sat down at my other side, pressing a kiss to my shoulder. I snuggled between my two men. Thinking about how happy I was, how much better my life was now than it had been even a year ago, just about broke my brain. How was it even possible?

But here I was, for real, with no murderous parents taunting me from the sidelines and no lingering fears that the rest of the fearmancers would never really accept me. With a life I'd chosen and built for myself, and two men who wanted nothing more than to share it with me.

We had each other and an immense future of possibilities ahead of us. And nothing about our happiness was an illusion now.

Eva Chase lives in Canada with her family. She loves stories both swoony and supernatural, and strong women and the men who appreciate them. Along with the Royals of Villain Academy series, she is the author of the Flirting with Monsters series, the Moriarty's Men series, the Looking-Glass Curse trilogy, the Their Dark Valkyrie series, the Witch's Consorts series, the Dragon Shifter's Mates series, the Demons of Fame Romance series, the Legends Reborn trilogy, and the Alpha Project Psychic Romance series.

*Connect with Eva online:*
www.evachase.com
eva@evachase.com